Deidre's Desires

D M Gaines

New Flavor
Books

Books by D M Gaines

Hood to Hood: A Cleveland Story
Hood to Hood 2: Spank's Revenge
Tiffany's Addiction: Director's Cut
All Flavors: A Book of Erotic Short Stories
Deidre's Desires
Hitting' Licks
Murder or Justice
Gemini Killer

Dedication

This book is dedicated to all of the women out there who are not scared to pursue and satisfy their sexual desires.

Acknowledgements

I would like to acknowledge and thank all of the following people. Fred Roberson, Micheal West and Big Twin thanks for being my critics. Beverly and Kevin Johnson thank you two for your support and making sure that my name lives on. To my coauthor Tiffany Rucker, I told you that we could do it. Victoria Johnson and Veronica Thompson thank you for your support. Last but not least, to all of you the ones that have purchased my books, thank you.

Sincerely Donny G

Chapter 1

Deidre always had strange urges since she was a kid. For years she fought to suppress those urges.

As early as the age of twelve, Deidre found herself experiencing different types of sexual urges. She often found herself staring at the other girls in the school's locker room as they changed into their cheerleading outfits.

On the weekends she would sleep over at her friend Karen's house. Karen had two brothers Derrick and Darnell. They would play two types of games during the weekend. One being house, in which Deidre would play the wife and Derrick would play the father with Karen and Darnell playing the kids. Derrick liked playing the husband because he and his wife would do everything that a real married couple would do. Derrick and Darnell would often argue over who would play the role of the husband.

One weekend things changed, when they were having their weekly argument, "I want to be the husband this week!" Darnell yelled at Derrick.

"I'm going to be the husband." Derrick responded.

"You always get to be the husband. I never get to get any. I'm going to tell mommy what you be doing to her."

"You do, and I will kick your ass." Derrick threatened.

Deidre did not want to chance any of them getting into trouble, so she came up with the solution, "Both of you can be my

All of a sudden Deidre got an overwhelming urge to taste Dianna, which she did. She put her whole month over Dianna's vaginal area and began sucking on it.

A horrifying sensation went through Dianna's body. She couldn't understand the feeling. She quickly shoved Deidre off of her and jumped up.

"What's wrong?" Deidre asked her.

"You are gross!" Dianna responded as she scrambled into her clothes and left in a hurry.

Ÿ

Later that evening, there was a knock at Deidre's bedroom door, "Come in," she said. The door opened and in walked her mother and father. Her father came into the room last, closed the door then leaned back on it. Deidre sat up in her bed, knowing that something was up.

Her mother spoke, "Dianna and her mother just left here and Dianna is accusing you of doing some awful things to her. I am going to ask you for your side of the story, so that I can get a better understanding as to what happened. So why don't you tell me what happened."

"Nothing happened we were doing research for our biology class."

"She said that you put your mouth on her vagina is that true?"

"Yeah it's true," her mother was shocked and could not believe her ears. Her father just stood there stoned face.

"What the hell is wrong with you Deidre? Why would you do something like that, are you crazy?"

"I just got the urge to do it."

"You just got the urge to put your mouth on another female's vagina, Earl do you hear this shit?" her father just shook his head, "Let me ask you a question Deidre, do you like boys or girls?"

"What do you mean?"

"I mean are you attracted to boys or girls dammit!"

"I like them both I guess."

"Are you crazy? Girls are not supposed to like other girls. It is wrong and it goes against God's word. I never want to hear about you engaging in that type of behavior ever again do I make myself clear?"

Deidre put her head down and said, "Yes,"

Her mother and father left her room and went back to theirs, "So what do you think?" her mother asked her father.

"I think she is just going through puberty and a phase that she will eventually grow out of."

"I think that we may need to get her some help. I can't remember at any age wanting to put my mouth on another woman's vagina."

"No, but you have always loved putting your mouth on this," Deidre's father said to her mother as he pulled his penis out of his pajamas. Deidre's mother put a wicked smile on her face as she approached him.

Chapter 2

The next day at school Deidre felt all of the stares and heard all of the giggles as she walked through the school's hallways. Some kids yelled slurs at her, "Carpet muncher!"

"Butch dagger!" Deidre knew that Dianna had spread the word about what she had done. None of her friends spoke to her at all that morning. At lunch she was sitting at a table all by herself until her friend Kayla came over and sat with her.

"Why are you over here?" Deidre asked her.

"Because, I don't care if you like coochie, you are still my friend. Tell me though, what did it taste like?"

Deidre felt embarrassed and got up from the table. When she got home from school, she went up to her room, laid down and started crying.

Deidre felt humiliated and confused. She did not understand why she got the type of urges that she was having. She did not know why she found herself attracted to the same sex. What she did know was that she had to learn how to control her urges and how to act normal if she wanted to be accepted by her peers.

As time went on things became back to normal for Deidre. The ridicule had stopped and even her friends had started to come back around. As time went on the whole incident had been forgotten by everyone except for Dianna.

Dianna would give Deidre menacing stares whenever they would be in the same vicinity.

Deidre was glad that things were back to normal, even though she did not feel normal. She suppressed her desire for women, but another one arose. Deidre found herself being attracted to voyeurism. She found that it excited her to watch other people having sex. She started her peep show at home, by sneaking and watching her parents while they had sex. Also she would sneak and watch her older brother June have sex with the girls that he would bring to the house while their parents were at work.

One time at school she hid on the bleachers and watched a group of guys from the football team take turns with one of the cheerleaders behind the bleachers. After watching the acts she would often head to her room and fantasize while she played with herself until she would cum.

Chapter 3

By the time that Deidre was a senior in high school, she had developed into a beautiful young woman. She was one of the prettiest girls in the school and all the boys would drool over her when she had on her cheerleading uniform.

Dianna was on the cheerleading squad also, and she often tried to turn the other cheerleaders against Deidre by telling them what she had done to her when they were kids.

The other girls would just wave Dianna off, thinking that she was just jealous of Deidre and all the attention that she was getting.

None of them believed that a girl as pretty as Deidre could be a bull dagger. Secretly, Dianna was having a hard time with her own sexuality. She did not want to admit to herself that what Deidre had done to her that day, had felt so good that it had scared her. She knew that it was wrong for a girl to feel what she had felt. It had felt so good that it had scared her and that is why she reacted the way she did.

Ever since that day Dianna had felt confused, because she would often have thoughts and fantasies about having sex with women. She had even recently started to find herself attracted to Deidre. She hated Deidre for the confusing feelings that she was having.

Deidre was trying her best to live a normal life. She had an after school job at Burger King and she had a steady boyfriend named Roger. She and Roger did lots of things together, but she liked it best when he took her over to his house.

Roger had a twin sister name Renee, and Deidre secretly found herself attracted to her.

She would always offer to do Renee's hair, so that she could sit between her legs. She would always make comments while doing her hair, "Girl your hair smells so fresh. I like the scent of that perfume that you are wearing." Renee always got a funny feeling when Deidre was around.

When she would sit between Deidre's legs to get her hair done, she would get a tingling sensation, and the hairs on her arms would stand up whenever Deidre's hands would make contact with her skin. She did not know where the feeling came from or what it meant, and she never spoke on it.

Roger was glad that his girl and his sister got along so good. They became almost like best friends. They would talk on the phone for hours at a time, and go out on the weekends to do shopping and attend movies.

One particular day they were in Renee's bedroom. Deidre was doing Renee's hair after which they were supposed to go shopping at the mall.

Deidre was sitting on the bed, while Renee sat on the floor in between her legs. Deidre was combing her hair when a ball of hair fell onto her shirt. Deidre reached down to wipe the hair off and her hand accidently rubbed across Renee's breast. A shock of electricity shot through Renee's body causing her to jerk, "I'm so sorry" Deidre said to her, rattled by what had just happened.

"Oh, it's okay," Renee told her as she wondered why her nipples had become hard. Something had passed through them, she was just unsure as to what it was.

Deidre finished her hair, and Renee decided to take a shower before they headed to the mall, "Girl put a movie in or some music on. I'm about to jump into the shower right quick." Renee told Deidre as she began stripping out of her clothes.

Deidre tried hard not to look at Renee as she undressed, but she could not help herself. She discreetly watched as Renee stripped down to her panties and bra.

She was amazed at Renee. She might have been Roger's twin sister but they certainly did not look alike, and definitely were not built alike.

Renee was the color of honey and had the looks of a young Anita Baker, but she had body like Lisa Raye had in Player's Club. Deidre's mouth started to water when she seen how full and round Renee's breast was. Renee grabbed a towel and headed out of the bedroom.

Deidre observed how round and full her ass was as she walked out of the room. Deidre sat there battling her emotions. She found that she was highly attracted to Renee and wanted to make a move. In her mind she weighed the consequences of what would happen if Renee rejected her advance and told Roger. She sat on the floor in front of the entertainment system and looked through the DVD collection. She found one that she thought she would like and put it into the player.

The rolling credits had just ended and the movie was about to start, when Renee came back into the room. She was wearing nothing but a towel and her body was still glistening wet. She walked over to her dresser and began picking through bottles of body lotions and perfumes. After she gathered an armful of cosmetics, she walked over to the bed and flopped down on it. When she flopped down the towel that she had wrapped around her folded over to one side leaving her pelvic area exposed.

"Girl, what are you watching?" Renee asked her. When Deidre turned around she was eye level with Renee's hairy bush. Renee's pussy was covered with thick, dark, curly hair and Deidre could not take her eyes off of it.

Renee noticed how hard Deidre was staring between her legs and straightened the towel out.

"What are you watching girl?" she asked Deidre again snapping her out of her trance.

"Oh ... Uh ... Uh, I put in Jennifer's body." Deidre responded.

"Ain't that the movie where Megan Fox and that other white girl Amanda Seyfrieds are lovers?"

"Yeah that's it."

"I wonder what two women get out of licking each other. I mean how could they cum without any dick being involved?" Renee stated as she started to lotion up. Deidre did not know how to answer that question without getting herself into trouble, so she just remained quiet.

"Shit I can't ever get to the middle of my back. Would you mind putting some of this lotion on my back for me?" Renee asked Deidre.

"No, I don't mind." Deidre replied as she stood up, removed her shoes and walked over to the bed. She climbed onto the bed behind Renee and took the bottle of lotion from her.

She squirted some of the lotion into one of her hands then rubbed both of her hands together. She put the palms of her hands onto Renee's back and started rubbing the lotion.

Renee felt a cool sensation that was soon replaced by a warm sensation. Deidre's hands came up to her shoulders and the tips of her fingers started to dig into Renee's shoulder blades. Renee closed her eyes and let out a slight moan. Deidre dug the tips of her fingers in further, "Just relax," she told Renee.

Deidre grabbed the lotion bottle and squirted some more onto her hands.

"Okay lay flat down." she told Renee.

Renee turned onto her stomach and laid flat out on the bed. Deidre straddled her across her waist and began rubbing lotion into Renee's arms. Afterwards, she grabbed the bottle and squirted drops of lotion from the middle of Renee's back down to the crack of her ass.

She used her finger tips, thumbs and knuckles to knead into her flesh. She did that all the way down to her feet.

Renee's body was on fire. She had never felt the type of feelings that she was having before.

She did not know if she should stop Deidre or let her keep going. She knew that what was happening was wrong, but it felt so good.

All of a sudden she felt a cool sensation on her big toe. She turned her head to look behind her and seen that Deidre had her eyes closed while sucking on her toe. She was using her hands to massage her foot as she sucked her toe.

Renee just stared at her in amazement. When Deidre opened her eyes they locked in with Renee's. Both of their eyes were filled with lust.

Deidre removed Renee's toe from her mouth and helped her to roll over onto her back, then she started to devour her breast. First it was one at a time then both.

"Oh God, what are yon doing to me?" Renee asked.

"Shush, just relax," Deidre told her as she moved down between Renee's legs. She spread her legs out as far as they would go. She looked at her fat pussy lips, which looked moist. She took two fingers from her right hand and separated her pussy lips. Renee's pussy was already secreting a thick white substance and her clit was fully erect.

Deidre put her mouth down to her pussy and blew on her clit, and Renee's body started to tremble. Deidre put her mouth on Renee's mound. Renee used both of her hands to grip the sheets. She lifted her ass up off of the bed pushing her pussy further into Deidre's mouth. Deidre put her hands under Renee's ass and held her ass up in the air as she sucked her pussy.

All of a sudden Renee's body started flopping around like a fish out of water, and then her body went rigid. Her feet pointed straight out as an orgasm violently ripped through her body. She took both of her hands and placed them on Deidre's head holding it in place as she came in her mouth. All of a sudden they heard Roger's voice coming from downstairs.

Chapter 4

Roger entered the house and called out to Renee, "Renee has Deidre called?"

"Oh, shit!" Deidre said as she jumped up. Renee did not seem fazed; she did not even get up and put her clothes on.

Deidre thought quickly. She heard the footsteps coming up the stairs and ran out of the room towards the steps, "hey baby," she said to Roger as he rounded the steps.

"Hey, how long have you been here?"

"Only for about twenty minutes. I just got done doing Renee's hair." Roger noticed a white substance around the corners of Deidre's mouth, "You got something on the corner of your mouth," Deidre quickly put her hand up to her face and wiped her mouth. She stuck her fingers into her mouth and sucked the substance off.

"Oh, that was the glaze off of a Danish I ate," Deidre said with a smile.

"Well come on to my room, I'm hungry for you."

They went into Roger's room, where Roger grabbed Deidre and they both fell onto the bed. They started tongue kissing. Roger noticed that she had a sweet and tangy taste in her mouth. It was an unusual taste, but one that he had tasted many times before. He just couldn't recall where he tasted it.

"That Danish must have been real tangy" he said as he stood up began stripping out of his clothes.

"It was a glazed lemon Danish," she replied as she also began to take her clothes off.

She laid back on the bed and spread her legs wide. Roger climbed on the bed and got on top of her. He started kissing her on her neck and nibbling on her ear. Those things usually got Deidre hot, but for some reason she wasn't responding to them.

He worked his way down to her breast and then to her navel. Deidre closed her eyes and started imagining that he was his sister. She grabbed his head and pushed down further. He tried to stop at her navel but she kept pushing until his face was leveled with her pussy.

Roger flicked his tongue out and sent shockwaves through her body. He started eating her pussy as if it was his dinner and he hadn't eaten all day.

Deidre had her eyes closed fantasizing about Renee. When she got to the point of no return, she screamed out the wrong name out, "Yes Renee make me cum," Roger thought he had heard wrong but again he heard her say, "Yes Renee I'm cumming."

Roger stopped eating her out and stood up, "What the fuck! You in here fantasizing about my sister, are you a dike?" Deidre sat up with a confused look on her face, "Huh, what are you talking about?" she asked him.

"You might be deaf but I ain't. I asked you were you fantasizing about my sister sucking your pussy? You just called her name out twice while I was doing it."

"Boy, you are tripping I ain't said Renee's name."

"I know what the fuck I heard. You two have been hanging pretty tight. Are y'all diking?"

"You got me fucked up! I ain't no dike. You are acting real insecure, like you are jealous of your sister."

"Bitch! I ain't never been insecure. I'm going to holla at my sister though." Roger threw his pants on and left out of the room. He walked down to Renee's room and barged right in. Renee was lying naked asleep in the exact same spot that Deidre had left her in.

"Renee!" Roger yelled startling her out of her sleep.

Renee jumped up and tried to cover up, "Boy what is wrong with you just busting in my room like that?"

"Fuck that, is you and that bitch Deidre diking?"

"What did you say?"

"I said is you and that bitch Deidre diking?"

"Are you crazy? I ain't no damn dike!"

"She sure called your name out twice while we were together a few minutes ago." Roger noticed Renee was looking over his shoulder. He turned and seen that Deidre was standing in the doorway.

"You two are trying to play me like I'm crazy. You up in here naked she just left your room, she calling your name out." Deidre and Renee locked eyes for a second, and then Renee turned away.

"I don't know what you are talking about. You are my brother first off and second I don't like girls."

"Well, something is up with you two. I know what I heard, so I'm going to leave the two of you here to work it out!" Roger said then stormed out of the room.

Renee looked at Deidre, who was still standing in the doorway.

"Fuck you standing there for? This shit is your fault. I ain't gay and I shouldn't have let you do that to me."

"Yeah right, you liked it just as much as I did. The cum that, you left around my mouth proves it."

"Well it's never going to happen again, and I'm going to deny that it happened until the day that I go to my grave. Now get out! Just go!" Deidre turned and slowly walked out of the room. She walked back to Roger's room to get her purse and found that he had left. She grabbed her purse and left also.

Renee crashed onto her bed and started crying. She knew that what had happened with her and Deidre was wrong. She had never done anything like that before, and could not understand why she had let it happen.

All she knew was that it felt good, real good. She had never experienced any of the sensations that she had felt with Deidre with any man.

She knew that she was going to have to deal with her brother and the conflicting feelings that she was having within herself.

Chapter 5

Dianna had been going through mood swings lately, which was putting her at odds with her boyfriend Fred. One minute she would be warm and receptive to him and then the next she would act cold towards him and shut him out.

Sometimes they would be having sex and she would just start crying for no apparent reason. He would ask her what was wrong and she would just tell him to get up.

Then one day Dianna just up and told him, "I think we should take a break from each other for a while."

"What the hell do you mean take a break? Why you are tripping, you fucking someone else or something?"

"No, I ain't fucking nobody else. I'm just going through some things that I need to work out."

"Di, I'm your man, I'm supposed to help you out with anything that you are going through."

"You can't help me with what I am going through. After I figure everything out, you will be the first person that I talk to, but until then I need space."

"Yeah okay, I will give you your space, but I will tell you that I'm not going to put my life on hold forever waiting for you to figure things out."

"I don't want you to put your life on hold. If it is meant for us to be together, we will find our way back into each other's lives." Fred just gave up and left.

Dianna thought to herself, "It's time to find out are these feelings real or not." she grabbed her car keys, went and jumped into her car and headed up to Burger King.

She pulled into the drive through line at Burger King and heard a familiar voice come through the speaker, "May I take your order please?"

"Yes, give me a whopper with cheese and a chocolate shake."

"That will be $3.79 at the window."

"Okay, thank you," Dianna said then pulled around to the window. The cashier opened the window to collect the payment, and was surprised to see that it was Dianna, with a serious look on her face. Dianna said, "Deidre we need to talk." Deidre did not know how to take that statement. She and Dianna had not talked since they were twelve years old. Now here it was she was seventeen and pulled up to her place of employment was Dianna saying that they needed to talk.

"Okay, when do you want to talk?"

"How about I come over to your house tomorrow after school?"

"That will be fine," Deidre told her as she handed her the order. Dianna grabbed the items and pulled off.

Deidre was hoping that there wouldn't be any drama. She was already going through enough as it was. Roger had an attitude with her and ignored her at school. Then, Renee would call her phone, and yell into it, "You fucked my life up," then hang up.

Deidre had no idea what that was about. She figured that she might as well brace herself for some more drama the next day.

Chapter 6

The next day around 4:30pm, Deidre was up in her room doing some homework, when the doorbell rang. She went downstairs to answer it. When she opened the door there stood Dianna. She was wearing a short mini skirt and a sheer blouse. She stood at the door fidgeting with her purse.

"Come on in, I was just doing a little homework." Dianna stepped in and Deidre closed the door.

Deidre led the way up to her room. They entered it and Dianna got flashbacks. The room looked exactly as it did five years before and it brought back memories. Deidre sat down on her bed and told Dianna, "You can sit in that chair if you want." Instead of moving to the chair, Dianna took a seat on the edge of the bed and said, "This will be fine."

They just sat there staring at each other for a few minutes, before Deidre broke the ice, "So what do you want to talk about?"

"You know what you did to me messed me up don't you?"

"Dianna, we were kids and nothing really happened."

"Something happened, because I have been questioning my sexuality ever since that day."

"What do you mean?"

"Sometimes I find myself being attracted to women, and sometimes I fantasize about having sex with them, you included."

"And you blame me for that?"

"The feeling that you gave me that day, I haven't felt it since, and it seems like I have been on an endless searched trying to find it. I can't even get intimate with my boyfriend. I wonder if having sex with a woman will bring that feeling back."

"So, what exactly are you saying Dianna?"

"I'm saying that I want you to make love to me, so that I can know if I am straight or gay." Deidre couldn't believe what she was hearing.

"Okay and what if you find out that you are gay or bisexual then what?"

"Then I will take it from there," Dianna said then stood up and started removing her clothing.

Deidre just sat there and watched her. When Dianna unhooked the clasp on her bra and her breast burst free, Deidre just stared at them taking in how beautiful they were. They were perfect in every way, size, shape and the way that they sat up. She had big dark nipples that stuck out almost half an inch.

When she stepped out of her skirt, Deidre seen that she was wearing a thong, Dianna stood facing her and Deidre could see her pussy lips straining to be free of the fabric that held them hostage. Deidre's mouth started to water as Dianna started pulling down her thong. "Turn around," she said to Dianna as she pulled the thong down.

Dianna obliged by turning around and slowly stepping out of her thong.

Dianna had one of the most beautiful asses that Deidre had ever seen. There was not one mark or blemish on it. There was no sign of any discoloration. Deidre found herself breathing deeply.

She stood up and walked over to Dianna. She put her hands on the back of her neck and pulled her to her. They engaged in a long tongue kiss. Dianna brought her arms up and put them on Deidre's back as their tongues dug deeper into each other's mouth.

Dianna felt her nipples start to stiffen and her heart rate started to go up. Excitement started to fill her body.

Deidre broke the kiss, pushed Dianna onto the bed and was about to advance on her, when through deep breaths Dianna said, "Take your clothes off." Deidre started undressing as Dianna watched on.

Seeing Deidre strip caused a wetness to appear between Dianna's legs. Right then she realized that she was indeed attracted to women.

She was shocked when Deidre stepped out of her panties and she seen that her pussy was completely bald. She instantly wondered what it tasted like.

Deidre crawled onto the bed and between Dianna's legs. Dianna opened her legs wide, inviting her. Deidre laid on top of her. They were chest to chest and pussy to pussy.

They resumed the kissing after which Deidre slid down to her breast. She tended to each one of them individually, making sure to give each one of them the same amount of attention. She used both hands to hold onto one as she sucked and licked it. She gently nibbled on her nipple sending sparks through Dianna's body.

"Oh God!" Dianna moaned.

After finishing with her breast, Deidre took the tip of her tongue and made a trail all the way down past her navel to her pussy.

She took her thumb and forefinger from her left hand and spread open Dianna's pussy lip and used two from her right hand to enter her. She first went in a circular motion at the entrance to her pussy. Her fingers quickly became coated with a sticky white substance. She pushed the two fingers inside of Dianna and moved them around in a rhythm. After she got her fingers coated, she removed them from Dianna's pussy and stuck them into her mouth and tasted them. To her they tasted like honeysuckle, "umm," she moaned as she licked her fingers clean.

She then put her mouth on Dianna's pussy, "There it is," Dianne said to herself as that feeling from five years ago started to come back.

Deidre concentrated on the top of her mound, sucking her clit area. Even though her pussy lips were closed, her clit stuck out like an animal sticking its head out of the bushes in the forest.

Deidre put her full concentration on it. She gently sucked and nibbled on it.

The feeling was so great that it was almost too much to bear. She reached behind her and grabbed a pillow. She pulled the pillow down to her face and bit into it as her body started to convulse.

From the way that her thighs started to tremble, Deidre knew that she was cumming. She stuck her two fingers back inside of Dianna and started to finger fuck her in a fast rhythm.

Dianna violently shook her head from side to side as another orgasm ripped through her body. She had never in her life experienced multiple back to back orgasms.

She threw the pillow onto the floor and rose up to look at how Deidre was finger fucking her and eating her pussy at the same time. She didn't know what made her blurt the words out of her mouth. It was as if they just came out on their own when she said, "I love you Deidre. Damn I love you." Deidre rolled off of her and onto her back. She grabbed her knees and pulled them back then said, "Show me."

Dianna did everything to Deidre that she had done to her, starting with her breast. When she got to Deidre's pussy she attacked it like a tiger attacking a deer. To her it came naturally. She had Deidre in ecstasy bringing her to her second climax, when Deidre's bedroom door opened and in walked her mother,

"Deidre!" she said as she went into the room. She stopped when she seen the two figures on the bed.

Dianna rolled over onto the floor on the other side of the bed, trying to hide.

"Hell no! Hell fucking no! I knew that you needed help. Earl get up here and Dianna get your nasty ass up. Wait until I tell your mother this with your little Ms. Innocent ass. Get your ass up and put your clothes on, you too Deidre."

Deidre's father came to the door, "What's going on?"

"What's going on, your daughter and the same damn girl that claimed that she molested her years ago, were just on that bed naked doing it to each other!"

"Carolynn, calm down, you are hyper ventilating."

"What the hell do you mean calm down. Our daughter is up here bumping coochies with another girl and you want me to calm down? I ought to beat the devil out of her!" she said then charged at Deidre.

Deidre was not prepared for her mother's actions and could not get out of the way in time before her mother got a hold of her. Her mother grabbed her by the hair and started hitting her up side her head with her open hand.

Dianna wasn't even fully dressed, but rushed to the door with the rest of her clothing in her arms. Deidre's father stepped aside to let her pass, and then stepped over to intervene between his wife and daughter.

"Carolynn that's enough! Stop it!" he told her as he tried to pull his wife off of his daughter.

Carolynn had a fistful of her daughter's hair, and held onto it as her husband tried to pull her off of Deidre. Deidre struggled to break free, but her mother had a firm grip.

"You got the devil in you! You need help, I'm going to beat it out of you!" she yelled at Deidre.

Deidre's father started prying his wife's fingers off of Deidre's hair.

"Let her go Carolynn, I'm not going to ask you again!" he told her raising his voice.

Deidre's mother reluctantly let go of her hair, "You always take up for her, take up for her somewhere else! I want her out of this house. As long as she is living that type of lifestyle, she is not welcomed in this house!" Deidre's mother said then stormed out of the room.

She went downstairs, grabbed her keys off of the coffee table, went out and got into her car, then headed towards Dianna's house.

Deidre was laying on her bedroom floor in a fetal position crying. Her father went and helped her up onto the bed, "It's going to be okay sweetheart. She is just upset right now. Just give her some time, she will come around." Deidre hugged her father and put her head on his shoulder.

"Let it out, everything is going to be okay. Get yourself together, and then we will talk okay?" In between sniffles Deidre told her father, "Okay,"

"I will be waiting for you downstairs" he told her then left the room, so that she could get herself together.

Chapter 7

Deidre's mother pulled into Dianna's parent's driveway and parked behind Dianna's car. She got out of her car and marched up to the door and started pounding on it.

Dianna's mother came running from the kitchen to see who the hell it was that was banging on her door like a fool, "Who is it?" she asked as she approached the door.

"It's Carolynn!"

"Carolynn!" Dianna's mother quickly snatched her front door open, "Are you crazy? Why the hell are you banging on my door like that?"

"Who is that Kathy?" Dianna's father asked from the top of the steps.

"It's Deidre's mother Carolynn." After hearing who it was, Dianna's father retreated back to his study room. Dianna was in the shower at the time and did not hear the commotion.

Carolynn barged into the house, "Where is that little tramp?"

"First off, who are you referring to, second please lower your tone, and third what is your problem?" Dianna's mother asked her as she started to get upset.

"I'm referring to little Ms. Innocent as you would call her, your daughter."

"Wait a damn minute, don't you come up in my house disrespecting anyone in my family."

"Your daughter is a pussy eater. You accused my daughter of being one years ago, without any evidence. Well, I witnessed firsthand today your little trifling daughter with her head between my daughter's legs going to town, and she looked like a real professional."

"Carolynn, I can clearly see that you are upset, but I am going to ask you one more time to stop disrespecting my child."

"Fuck you and your child!" Dianna's mother had taken enough, she rushed forward swinging her arms in the windmill fashion. Carolynn tried to back pedal and tripped. She tried to catch herself by reaching out to grab hold to something. She grabbed hold of a lamp that was on an end table. The lamp went crashing to the floor right along with her.

The lamp hit the floor and shattered. That startled Dianna, who was up in her room getting dressed. Her father had heard the noise to and ran out of the study. Both he and Dianna reached the steps at the same time. He took off down the stairs while Dianna stood there shocked at what was going on.

Dianna's mother and Deidre's mother were both on the floor tussling, "Stop it you two!" he yelled as he ran over to break them up. He called for Dianna, "Come help me break them apart." Dianna came running down the steps, but when she got to them instead of breaking them up she started hitting Deidre's mother in her face, "Get off my mother bitch!" she yelled at Carolynn as she hit her in her face.

"Dammit Dianna, you stop that now!" her father screamed at her. Dianna ignored her father and kept striking Carolynn. Her father advanced on her, and grabbed her. He shook her violently,

"My God what the hell is wrong with you?" Take your behind up to your room right now!" he turned her towards the stairs and pushed her in that direction. When she made it to the steps, he turned his attention back to his wife and Carolynn, both of whom were both on their feet, but had a fist full of each other's hair, "Stop it you two, before I break both of your two fingers," he told them as he started prying their fingers from each other's head.

He finally got them free of each other, at which time Carolynn headed for the door yelling, "This ain't over bitch!"

"You bring your ass back over here again and you're going to get your ass kicked again bitch!" Dianna's mother screamed after her.

"Kathy calm down, and tell me what happened between you two."

"She just came over here banging on the door and when I opened it, she started calling Dianna all kinds of insults and said that she caught Dianna and Deidre naked in bed."

"The two of you couldn't have a civil conversation?"

"Aren't you listening to me?"

"Yes, I'm listening."

"The woman just barged in here and started ranting and raving. I asked her twice to settle down and she wouldn't. What was I supposed to do, just continue to let her disrespect me and my child in my home?"

"Your right, I'm sorry. Let's go upstairs and have a talk with Dianna. We need to see what all of this is about." They headed upstairs to have a talk with Dianna.

Ÿ

At the same time Deidre and her father were having a talk.

"So you are gay?" her father asked her.

"I guess, I mean I like boys too. I love Roger, but for some reason I'm also attracted to girls sexually. Does that make me a bad person?"

"No it doesn't make you a bad person. It makes you different, but not bad."

"So, are you going to hate me the way mom does?"

"Your mother doesn't hate you, and I surely do not hate you. Your mother is a very religious person and the Bible preaches against such behavior. If this is you then your mother is going to have to eventually come around. You are our child and no matter what your sexual preference might be, we are still going to love you as our child. You are my baby girl and I love you unconditionally. I'm going to have a talk with your mother, but please do not flaunt that type of behavior in her face until she is able to deal with it. Now go on back up to your room."

Chapter 8

Dianna's parents went up to her room and questioned her about what happened. Dianna explained to them the feelings and mixed emotions that she had been experiencing since the incident that had happened five years earlier.

"Let me get this straight for five years you have been questioning your sexuality?" her mother asked her.

"Yes,"

"What about Fred?"

"I broke up with Fred, because of the feelings and urges that I was having to be with a woman."

"What was your purpose for going over there and doing what you did?"

"I needed to find out, if I am indeed gay."

"So Dianna what is your conclusion?" asked her father.

"I know that I am sexually attracted to women, but I do not know if there is anything beyond that. I don't know if I can be in a relationship with a woman as I could with a man."

"Listen Di, we are going to love you no matter what. You be careful though, because you could end up hurting people including yourself in the process. You just can't go around experimenting with people trying to find yourself. If you think that you may need some counseling, we can get you some, do you hear me?"

"Yes,"

"Now come and give me and your mother a hug." Dianna walked over and got embraced by each of her parents.

It was a big relief to know that she had their support. She now knew that she liked having sex with women. Now she needed to know if it went beyond that. If only she could figure out how to find that out.

Ϋ

When Deidre's mother got home, her husband was still sitting on the living room sofa. She entered the house and he looked up. His face turned into a mask of shock when he seen how disheveled her hair was, the bruises on her face, and how her clothes were ripped.

He jumped up off of the sofa and approached her, "Carolynn what happened to you?"

"That bitch Kathy and her slut daughter doubled teamed me."

"What! Tell me that you did not go over to them people's home and start trouble?"

"Whose side are you on? Dammit! Look at me!"

"Carolynn, this is not about taking no sides, it's about right and wrong, and you were dead wrong to go over to their house starting trouble." Carolynn got frustrated with how her husband was acting.

"Fuck them and fuck you too!" Carolynn stated angrily. She could not understand how he could sit up there and be so calm through the whole situation, "Where is that little devil? Is she out of this house yet?"

"Carolynn I am overlooking a lot of things right now because I know that you are upset, but know this, our daughter is not going any damn where. I do not care whatever it is she likes, she is my seed and I am going to stand by her. Your holier than thou ass need to grow up and realize that this is the 21ˢᵗ century."

"I don't give a damn what century it is, I'm not going to sit up here and allow my daughter to be no damn carpet muncher and I will not support her being one!"

"That's fine and dandy, but like I said she ain't going nowhere. She is about to graduate in two more months at which time she will be going off to college. Until then, she will be right here in this house. If you can't get along with her then you just let her be. I mean it Carolynn! You let her be." Carolynn had never seen her husband get so mad. She decided that it would be best to let the subject go for the time being, at least until she could figure something out.

Chapter 9

Roger and Renee had not been speaking in weeks and their mother started to take notice. They were having breakfast at the kitchen table and there was an eerie silence. Their mother had had enough.

"What is wrong with you two?" she asked them. Neither of them spoke, "I don't know what's going on, but you two need to get your act together. Roger why hasn't Deidre been around lately?" Roger looked over at Renee, who looked back at him.

"We aren't together anymore."

"What happened? She seems like such a nice girl."

"Or boy," he said with a smirk on his face.

"What did you say?"

"Nothing ma, we just decided to give each other some space for a while."

"Well, I hope that you two work things out. I know that I am tired of seeing you moping around here as if you lost your best friend. And you two walking around here giving each other the silent treatment is killing me. I know that you are twins and have the same attitude but my God you are brother and sister. You two need to work whatever it is out. Renee you clear the table and wash the dishes when you get in from school. I have to go before I am late for work." her mother told them, then walked out of the kitchen.

Later that day Roger was in the locker room at school. His basketball team had just finished having practice.

Him and three of his friends had just finished showering and were changing back into their clothes when his friend Tyrone asked, "What's up with you and Deidre, Roger? What she dumped you or something?" The rest of the boys started laughing at the crack.

"For your information I did the dumping."

"Okay then, return of the Mack!" his friend Mike said kidding.

"For you to dump somebody that bad, you must have hooked up with Megan Good." Tyrone said to him.

"Let's just get off of me right now. I don't feel like talking about that shit."

"Ooh, calm down lover boy!" Tyrone said to him. They finished getting dressed and headed out of the locker room going their separate ways.

Roger's close friend Billy, who stayed quiet through the whole ordeal in the locker room walked away with Roger.

It was lunch time and they headed to the cafeteria. They got their trays and went and set at a table over in the corner.

They were eating when Billy said, "You know that you are my boy and I care about you dawg. I got to tell you that you haven't been the same since you and Deidre broke up. Whatever happened had a deep effect on you. It is plain to see that you miss her though."

"Yeah, I miss her. That was my girl."

"If you don't mind me asking why did you two break up?"

"I think she is diking man."

"And why do you think that?" Roger thought for a moment. He figured it was better not to tell him exactly why.

"Let's just say she been doing things that indicate that she is or wants to." Billy got excited, "And you're tripping over that shit. I know you know that's every man's fantasy is to have a woman that likes women. The real catch is that women that like other women are going to bring women into bed with their man. Fuck is wrong with you, I thought you were a player. Man I wish I were in your shoes."

Roger sat there thinking about what had happened. He had never truthfully thought about which part he was actually mad about. Was it the fact that she liked women or that fact that it was his sister that she liked.

He did start to realize that he was over reacting.

"You're right dawg, I have been tripping. If we both like the same thing that's cool, as long as she ain't trying to cut me out."

"That's it dawg, bring that player shit back. You had me scared for a minute. I thought that I was going to have to revoke your player's card."

"I'm alright, good looking though dawg."

"That's what friends are for, now go and find your girl." They finished their lunch and Roger took off in search of Deidre. He knew that her next class would be Algebra, so he headed there.

At the second bell, Deidre came around the corner heading to her class. Her head was down, so she did not see Roger until she almost bumped right into him. She looked up into his face and realized how much she missed him and how much she cared for him.

Roger had a nervous smile on his face when he asked her, "How are you doing?"

"I'm alright I guess."

"Listen, I may have flew off of the deep end a little bit, well a lot, I just want to say that I am sorry and I want you to come over to the house after school to spend some time with me. Can you do that?"

Deidre instantly cheered up. She had really been missing him.

"Yeah I can do that, but I got to be to work by five o'clock."

"That's cool, I will meet you at your locker when school lets out."

Ÿ

When school let out Roger met Deidre at her locker and together they headed outside and climbed into his Ford truck.

They went to Roger's house, and when they entered Renee was sitting on the living room sofa watching television. When she seen her brother and Deidre enter the house she gave them a look that could kill.

Neither Roger or Deidre spoke to Renee. They headed upstairs to Roger's room, where neither of them hesitated to strip out of their clothes.

They met in front of the bed and Roger reached out and pulled Deidre to him. He embraced her, and both of their naked bodies exchanged warmth.

Roger put both of his hands on the side of Deidre's face and started kissing her. It was like he couldn't control himself. He was all over her to the point that he was making it hard for her to breathe.

Deidre had to break the embrace, "Slow down baby, I ain't going anywhere." Roger took deep breaths then said, "Sorry, I've just missed you so much." he started to advance on her again, but Deidre told him, "You let me take control, lay down on the bed." Roger fell back on the bed and Deidre climbed on top of him. She kissed him in the mouth, licked his ear and nibbled on his nipples. Roger's breathe deepened when she started heading down to his dick.

She did not hesitate to engulf him. His whole body shook as she took him all the way into her mouth.

Deidre used one of her hands to cuff his balls. She rolled his balls around in her hand like they were marbles as she sucked him off. Roger did not know how much longer he could take that kind of treatment.

Deidre could tell that he was becoming too sensitive from the tremors that she felt going through his body. She decided to give him an extra treat before she stopped.

She took his dick out of her mouth and put his balls into it. She started humming on his nuts sending a vibrating sensation throughout his whole body. The sensation was becoming so overwhelming that Roger actually took both of his hands and pried Deidre off of him.

"This is my show, don't run!" she told him as she pushed him back down and straddled him.

She squatted over him, reached down, grabbed his dick then slowly sank down on it.

To Roger, it was like sinking into a hot tub. Deidre sank all the way down on him, placed the palms of her hands on his wash board abs and began rotating her hips. She would switch positions, rotating to the right then, switching to the left. Roger had his eyes closed making fuck faces.

Outside of Roger's door, was Renee. She had tried to quietly open the door to see what they were doing, but the door was locked so she settled for putting her ear to the door to try and hear what was going on. She did not have to wait too long.

Roger could not take it anymore. He needed to be in control. He pushed Deidre off of him, rolled her over and pulled her up into the doggy style position. He started fucking her from the back. Actually he was not on his knees. He was squatting down over top of her with his hands on her hips.

He was slow stroking Deidre and she was loving it. One thing Roger made her realize was that she might like having sex with women, but she could never imagine giving up dick completely. She liked the way it filled her body up. Roger needed reassurance he needed Deidre to boost his confidence, so he started talking to her, "Whose pussy is this Deidre?" In between gasps Deidre responded, "It's yours Roger! All yours!"

"Tell me how you want it!"

"Hard, give it to me hard." Deidre grunted like a wild animal and started rocking back and forth on her knees to meet his thrust. She felt her climax approaching, "Shit! ... Fuck! Here it comes. Get it Roger! Get it!" Roger went full speed slamming into her. His balls made a loud slapping sound as they slammed up against the back of her thighs every time he rammed into her.

Outside of the door Renee had tears in her eyes. She had slid down to the floor with her head lying on the door.

She was starting to hate Deidre and her own brother. She wondered to herself, "Why can't that be me in there with her instead of him." She got up and went into the bathroom. She opened up the bathroom's medicine cabinet and took out a pack of Bic razors. She took one razor out of the pack and went back and sat outside of her brother's door.

Once Deidre and Roger were through sexing, she still had almost an hour before she had to be at work. They laid up in the bed talking for a minute.

"So where do we go from here?" she asked Roger.

"It depends on how truthful you be."

"Are you sure that you want the truth?"

"There is only one thing that I truly need to know."

"And what is that?"

"Do you like women?"

"To be totally honest, yes I do. I have been liking girls since I was twelve years old."

"Since you were twelve!"

"Yeah, since I was twelve."

"So, you have had sex with women before?"

"Yes, I have."

"Why haven't you ever told me this Deidre?"

"I don't know. It's not something that you just go around telling people, especially people that you care for. I have been dealing with this issue since I was a kid. I was shunned by people that I thought were my friends when I was younger. Me and my mother are not on speaking terms because she does not approve of me." Deidre could not hold back anymore. She let the tears run freely from her eyes at full force.

Roger reached over and pulled her to him, "It's okay," he told her as he kissed her on top of her head.

They heard a thud outside of Roger's door, "What was that?" Deidre asked him.

"I don't know!" Roger said as he got up off of the bed and pulled his pants on. Deidre got up and started picking her clothes up off of the floor.

Roger got to the door and opened it. Renee crashed to the floor. Blood covered the top half of her body, "Oh shit! Renee! Renee! What's wrong?" Deidre seen Renee laying on the floor covered in blood.

"Oh my God! What happened?"

"I don't know, but we got to get her to the hospital. Roger reached down and picked his twin sister up. She laid in his arms limp.

"Grab my car keys and let's go!" he yelled to Deidre, and then took off running downstairs. He had on nothing but a pair of pants. He had a hard time getting the door opened with Renee in his arms, but he managed it. He got out to the car but had to wait on Deidre to unlock the car. Deidre came running out of the house only half dressed herself. She held her blouse and shoes in one hand and his car keys in the other, "Open the door for me!" he said to her.

Deidre unlocked the car door, opened it and pulled the front seat forward.

Roger put Renee into the back seat and was about to get into the car when his mother pulled into the driveway behind him. She seen that he did not have a shirt on, so she thought that he was just grabbing something out of his car. Roger screamed at her to back up, but because her windows were up she didn't know what he was saying. He took off towards her car at which time she seen that his chest was covered with blood. She tried to get out of her car, but he did not let her get all the way out, "You have to move the car I got to get Renee to the hospital."

His mother started getting hysterical, "What happened to my baby, where is she?"

"Mom move the damn car!" he yelled at his mother. She got back in her car, started it and pulled out of the driveway. Roger pulled out behind her, threw the car in drive and headed for the hospital with his mother hot on his tail.

"Deidre, look and see where the blood is coming from!" Roger told her. Deidre turned around in her seat and looked at Renee stretched out on the back seat. One of her arms was hanging off the seat. Deidre seen what looked to be blood bubbling from Renee's wrist area.

"I think she cut her wrist!"

"Shit! What the hell is wrong with her? It has to be you Deidre. Something had to happen between the two of you!" Roger yelled as he sped through the city streets trying to get his sister to the hospital as fast as he could. Deidre just remained quiet.

There was one light left before the hospital and it was red. Roger sped through it with his mother right behind him.

He pulled into the emergency room parking lot and jumped out of the car. His mother jumped out of her car and ran into the hospital as Roger pulled his sister from the car.

As Roger was entering through the sliding doors, paramedics were heading his way with a rolling gurney.

His mother was screaming frantically, "Help her! Help my baby!" The paramedics took Renee out of Roger's arms and put her on the gurney. They quickly wheeled her into a trauma room and began to work on her. They found that she was still alive but had a weak pulse. It was apparent that she had lost a lot of blood. The emergency room doctor examined her and found that she had cut both of her wrists, just missing a main artery in one of them. He ordered a nurse to draw some blood to get her blood type. They hooked her up to a respirator, and fitted her with an IV to get some plasma into her system. They then cleaned her wrists and began to stitch them up.

Roger and his mother were out in the waiting room, where his mother started to vent. She directed her frustration at him, "What did you do to her?" she screamed at him as she ran over to him and started beating him in his chest. Roger grabbed her arms to stop her from pounding on his chest.

"I didn't do anything ma. I don't know what happened." He pulled his mother to him and held her tightly while she cried in his arms.

Chapter 10

Deidre was so distraught that she forgot about work and caught a cab from the hospital to her house. She went straight up to her room, locked her door and fell onto her bed.

She started crying as she reflected on all the trouble her desires had caused. Things were starting to become to overbearing for her. She wasn't even eighteen yet and her life was filled with drama.

Her mother, Dianna, Roger and Renee, she did not know how much more she could take. For a minute she contemplated suicide.

"Maybe I should be the one to kill myself. I should just end it all." She did not understand how her sexuality could cause so much trouble.

She couldn't wait to graduate the upcoming month, so that she could head off to college. She just wanted to get away from it all. She laid there on the bed and cried herself to sleep.

Ÿ

Renee sat up in the hospital's recovery room. They had to give her almost two full bags of blood. Her wrists had been stitched and bandaged up. They gave her a pain pill and a sedative and she was sleeping peacefully.

Roger had gone out to his car and grabbed his gym bag out of the trunk. He went into one of the hospital's restrooms and cleaned himself up. He put on a t-shirt and a pair of shoes that he had in the bag. When he went out to the car he had seen that Deidre was gone. He thought that maybe she had went to work. He called her job twice and they told him they she hadn't come in. He called to her house four different times and got no answer. He decided to go back upstairs and check on his sister.

He caught the elevator up to the sixth floor and walked down to the room that they had his sister in. Renee was lying up in the bed with her eyes open. Their mother spoke, "Renee, what's wrong baby, just tell me?" Tears started to silently run from the corners of Renee's eyes.

"Talk to momma baby, what could be so bad that it could make you want to hurt yourself?"

Roger stood there in the doorway watching his sister cry. He hated seeing his twin sister like that and he started to cry also. He thought to himself, "Something must have happened between the two of them."

He turned and walked back to the elevator. He was going to find Deidre, because they needed to have a talk.

He got into his car and drove over to Deidre's house. He pulled into their driveway, got out of the car and went up to their door and knocked on it.

Deidre's father answered the door, "Mr. Sanders is Deidre home?"

"I think she is up in her room. Come on in I will call her down for you." Roger followed Deidre's father into the house and into the living room. Her father called upstairs, "Deidre, you got company." He got no response, so he yelled upstairs again, "Deidre you got company!" After still not getting an answer he told   Roger to have a seat while he went up to get her. Roger sat down on the living room sofa.

Deidre's father headed up the steps. He got to Deidre's room and tapped on the door, "Deidre you in there." Through sniffles Deidre replied, "Yes,"

"You got company downstairs."

"I don't want to see anyone." Her father heard the sniffles and tried to open her door. He found that the door was locked.

"Open the door so that I can talk to you for a minute." Deidre got up off of her bed and went and unlocked her bedroom door, and then she went back over and flopped back down on her bed. Her father opened the door and stepped in. Deidre was lying on her bed in the dark. He turned the light on, "What's wrong honey?"

"Nothing,"

"Something has to be wrong, you're lying up here in the dark crying."

"I don't want to talk about it right now dad. Can you just please tell whoever it is that I do not feel good?"

"Okay, if that's what you want." He opened her door to step out, but turned and said to her, "Sweetheart don't forget that you can always talk to me about anything. So if you find that you do want to talk, you let me know okay?"

"Okay," Deidre's father shut her door and went back downstairs.

Deidre appreciated her father's support. Unlike her mother he really had been there for her. Deidre and her mother had not spoken two words to each other since the day that she had caught Deidre and Dianna together. Deidre wanted to talk to her father, but just did not know how to explain the situation to him. It still felt embarrassing to her to talk about those type of things with him.

Her father went back downstairs and told Roger, "I'm sorry Roger, but Deidre is not feeling well. You are going to have to see her some other time."

"Could you please tell her that I said to call me Mr. Sanders?"

"I will surely tell her," he told him as he escorted him to the door.

Roger got back into his car. He did not know what to think or how to feel. He started his car and headed back up to the hospital to check on his sister and mother.

Chapter 11

Dianna set out on a quest to figure out what it was that she wanted. She wanted to find out if her attraction to women went beyond sex.

She wanted to start dating women to see what became of it. She started going out to gay clubs to meet girls. She got a few girls' numbers, but there was one particular girl that sparked her interest. Her name was Amber, and she was of mixed descent. Her mother was white and her father was black, which accounted for her long brown curly hair and her emerald green eyes.

Amber was nineteen, and out of school. She worked for a telemarketing firm.

Amber had been openly gay for three years. She hid her true self until she was sixteen.

Her mother was a prostitute and her father was her mother's pimp. Both of her parents were on dope most of their lives. They barely paid attention to her. One of her mother's prostitute friends started molesting her when she was thirteen and they never took notice.

It wasn't as if Amber wasn't receptive. She came to enjoy the experiences. After those experiences, she had sex with two boys on different occasions and found that she felt nothing with them. It was sex with women that she found satisfying.

Amber had only been in one monogamous relationship with a woman. It did not last long, because Amber was very possessive and could become very violent.

She had a couple women that she considered to be her fuck partners. She also frequently attended a gay bar called *All Girls*, to meet new women to have flings with.

Amber was aggressive and always went after whatever it was that she wanted.

She was in the bar and seen Dianna standing over against the wall by herself. The first thing that caught her attention was the richness of Dianna's skin. Her skin was creamy chocolate and it was very smooth. Dianna also had a look of innocence about her.

Amber approached her, "Excuse me, but are you here by yourself?" she asked Dianna.

"Yeah, it's just me."

"What is your name?"

"It's Dianna,"

"Hi Dianna, I'm Amber." she extended her hand to Dianna and she shook it.

Dianna looked at Amber intently and found that she was very attractive. She could tell that she was mixed with something.

"Hi Amber,"

"Would you like a drink?" Dianna knew that she was under age and shouldn't be drinking, but she told her, "I'll take a Daiquiri." Amber walked over to the bar and ordered two drinks. She headed back over to Dianna and said, "How about we have a seat?"

"Okay," they both walked over and found an empty table and sat down. As they were sipping their drinks Amber asked Dianna, "So are you in or out?"

"In or out of what?"

"The closet?"

"I don't know what you mean." Amber thought to herself, "She really is green." She smiled then asked, "Are you openly gay?" Dianna started fumbling with her words. She had quickly found herself getting nervous,

"Uh, I really don't know what I am right now."

"So, you are really trying to find yourself?"

"Yeah, something like that."

"Have you ever got down before?" At that moment Dianna realized that women weren't any different than men when it came to picking up women. There it was she was sitting there talking to another woman that was coming on to her the same way that a man would.

She felt a little intimidated, "Only once," was her answer to Amber's question.

Amber was a little disappointed. She was hoping that she had stumbled upon a virgin. She wished that she could have been Dianna's first. She may not have been a virgin in the lesbian world but, only being with one person still made her fresh meat to Amber and she was on her like a predator.

"Dianna let me ask you this, are you here just chilling or are you looking? I'm asking you that because I find you attractive and I would like to get to know you better?"

"Honestly, I don't know what I'm doing, I don't even have any gay friends. I guess I'm ready to start dating women and see where it leads to."

"What do you think about me?" Amber asked her then stood up out of her seat. Dianna looked her up and down.

Amber was sexy to her. She had a set of perky titties, she had hips and ass that had to come from the black side of her family.

"I think you are pretty."

"Do you think that there is any chance that we could hook up and start dating?"

"We can see where things go."

"Okay lets exchange numbers, so that we can talk and hopefully we can get together this weekend to go out." They exchanged numbers, and then they both left the club at the same time. They got in their own cars and drove off heading in different directions.

Ÿ

The next day at cheerleading practice, Deidre did not practice the routine with the rest of the squad. She told the coach that she was not feeling well and he let her sit on the bleachers and watch the team practice.

Dianna could not concentrate, and kept messing up the routine, because she kept trying to watch Deidre.

She became so clumsy that the coach had to ask her was she on anything extra.

For some reason every time she looked at Deidre she got turned on.

After practice she walked over to the bleachers where Deidre was sitting. Deidre saw her approaching. She still had visions of them together in her head. She could look at her and her familiar taste would appear in her mouth. She said to Deidre, "Thanks Deidre." Deidre was confused and did not know what she was talking about.

"Thanks for what?"

"For showing me that I do like having sex with women. Well, at least I know that having sex with you was the bomb. I got to find out if I'm into woman altogether or is it just you that I am into."

"Well, I wish you well on your journey." Deidre said to her with a smile on her face.

"Say in the end I find that it is only you that I am attracted to sexually, then what?"

"We will deal with that then." Deidre told her then stood up and walked away.

The bell rang and Deidre left out of the gym heading to her next class. When she got there Roger was waiting for her. He was leaning up against the wall with his arms folded across his chest.

Deidre wasn't ready for the third degree that she knew he was about to give her. She quickly tried to steer the conversation, "How is Renee doing?"

"She cool, they gave her some blood and stitched her up. They still got her up there though. They got her under psychiatric observation."

"That's good that she is alright."

"Yeah physically, but mentally she is all screwed up, and I know that it has something to do with you. The two of you had sex together didn't you?" Renee hated lying to Roger. She thought about Renee's words, "I will deny it 'til the day that I go to my grave." She felt like she needed to do the same, "No Roger, we did not have sex."

"That's bull shit!" I'm not dumb Deidre."

"Roger please calm down. You are causing a scene and I have to go to class. I will talk to you later." Deidre headed into her class and Roger walked away frustrated.

Chapter 12

Amber and Dianna talked on the phone three nights in a row. They chatted like a regular girl and boy that was trying to get to know each other would do. They talked about everything from their favorite color to what their goals in life were.

Amber really knew how to woo her. Dianna liked her personality. She kept Dianna laughing.

They decided that they would go out Friday. Amber was going to pick Dianna up and they were going out to a club.

Friday came and Amber picked Dianna up.

Amber had a three series BMW. She handed Dianna a bottle of Corona when she got into the car, then turned her music up and pulled off.

Dianna thought that they were going to a gay club, but to her surprise Amber pulled up in front of a hip hop club. It seemed as if there was a party going on outside of the club. The sidewalks and streets were packed with people.

Amber pulled around to the back of the club and parked. They got out of the car and made their way back to the front of the club.

Amber paid the five dollars admittance fee for both of them.

When they entered the club the music was blaring full blast. *Shake your tail feather* by Nelly was blasting out of the speakers.

"Let's find a table." Amber yelled to her over the loud music. They walked to the back of the club and found a secluded table.

"What do you want to drink?" Amber asked Dianna.

"A strawberry …" Amber cut her off.

"Hold up! There will be no Kool-Aid drinking tonight, I know what to get you." Amber headed to the bar. She ordered herself a double shot of Tequila and ordered Dianna a double of straight Jack Daniels. Amber took to pills out of her purse. She put one into her mouth and crushed the other one up and put it in Dianna's drink. She used the straw, to stir the powdery substance up to help it dissolve.

She headed back over to their table and handed Dianna her drink. Amber took a seat and started sipping her drink. Dianna took a sip of her drink. When it hit the back of her throat she felt a burning sensation that carried on all the way down to the pit of her stomach.

"Yeah that's some strong shit! You have to gulp it down it in two shots!" Amber told her. Dianna took the glass put it up to her mouth and tipped her head back. She downed the drink in two gulps. She went into a fit of coughing and had to beat on her chest. Amber sat there laughing at her. The drink was so strong that Dianna never tasted the substance that Amber had put into her drink.

"You want to dance?" Amber asked her. Dianna was not ready to openly display her sexuality out in the open in a club full of straight people.

"I'm good right now." Amber did not even trip. She knew that it would only be a matter of time before the pill had Dianna rolling.

The club was very hot and stuffy Dianna started sweating. She was thirsty for something to drink again.

"You look like you need another drink?"

"Yeah, I'm getting real hot!" Dianna told her. Amber knew that the pill was kicking in along with that double shot of Jack Daniels. She knew that one of the side effects of ecstasy was the raising of your temperature.

"I will go get us some water," she told Dianna.

She went back over to the bar and ordered two large bottles of water. She headed back over to her table and seen that Dianna had already started to loosen up. She sat in her seat rocking back and forth to the beat of the music.

"Yeah, here she comes," Amber said to herself.

"Here drink this water," she handed the bottle to Dianna, who twisted the top off and turned the bottle up. When she took the bottle away from her mouth it was only half full.

Amber slid her chair over next to hers. She put her hand under Dianna's chin and lifted her face up until they were eye to eye. She told her, "You are so beautiful, I want to kiss you." She leaned in and kissed Dianna. At first Dianna was resistant to letting her tongue enter into her mouth. She eventually gave in and Amber's tongue found its way into her mouth.

Amber French kissed her as she used her hands to caress her breast. Dianna's body was on fire. She had never felt as hot as she was then. Also for some reason she felt real freaky. She put her hand up under Amber's skirt. She pulled her panties to the side and pushed three of her fingers inside of her. Amber spread her legs open so that Dianna could get all the way in her. Dianna was giggling, as she pushed her fingers in and out of Amber. Amber herself was rolling. She was super wet and horny. Dianna pulled her fingers from her pussy them put them to her mouth. She stuck all three of the fingers into her mouth and sucked them until there was nothing left on them.

The Lil John's song, *Get low* came on and Dianna said, "Ooh, that's my song!" All that about not wanting to show her sexuality went out of the door as she got up and grabbed Amber's hand.

"Come on let's dance." She led Amber to the dance floor, which was crowded. Dianna pushed her way through the crowded dance floor, until they were in the middle of it. She turned her back to Amber and started getting low. She used her hands to rub all over her.

Amber put her hands on her hips and started getting low with her. The other females in the club started looking at them with a disgusted look on their faces. The men started to cheer them on. A circle formed around them as people gave them room to put on a show.

Fred was in the club with his boy Rodney. They were standing at the bar sipping on drinks, when they saw the dance floor spreading out.

"Evidently someone is putting on a show in the middle of the floor. Let's go and see what's going on." Fred said to Rodney.

They headed over to the dance floor. They had to force their way through the crowd to see what was going on. When they got to the front, Fred seen who it was and his blood started to rise.

"Ain't that your bitch out there?" Rodney asked him.

"Man, that bitch told me that she needed space because she had some issues with herself that she needed to resolve. I guess this is what it was,"

"She like bitches dawg?"

"That's what it looks like. The bitch could have told me what was really up. We could have got down together." Fred said as he took off headed in Dianna's direction.

Rodney knew that his boy was about to trip and he wanted no parts of it, so he stayed where he was at.

Fred walked out onto the floor and grabbed Dianna's arm and started pulling her off of the floor.

"Hey, what are you doing?" Dianna asked him. She was so high she didn't even know who he was.

"You let her go!" Amber yelled at him.

"Bitch! Get your dike ass out of here before I fuck you up."

"You ain't go do shit to me! You got me fucked up." Amber took off towards her table to grab her purse.

Fred drug Dianna to the front door. Rodney seen the mixed girl running after them and knew that there was about to be trouble. He took off heading for the door.

Fred got Dianna outside and had her up against the wall. "So you sucking pussy now? You left me to be with a bitch?"

"Fred that's you?" Dianna asked giggling.

"Oh, you getting high now too? Fuck is wrong with you?"

"You let her go!" Amber said coming towards them.

When she got to them she grabbed Fred's arm. Fred took his free arm and mugged her.

"I told you to beat it bitch!" Amber stumbled to the ground, got up and went into her purse. Fred had Dianna by her arms shaking her as if he was trying to shake some sense into her. All of a sudden he felt a sharp pain shoot through his arm. He looked and seen that Amber had stabbed him and was about to do it again, when Rodney grabbed her wrist and twisted the knife out of her hand.

"You bitch!" Fred yelled as he used his good arm to put his hand around Amber's throat and started to choke her.

Rodney had to pull him off of her.

"Come on dawg, it's too many people out here. Somebody is going to call the police. It ain't worth it. Let me get you to the hospital. She got you leaking!"

"Dianna, you ain't shit you dike bitch!" Fred yelled to her as Rodney led him away.

Amber caught her breath and told Dianna, "Let's go." Dianna was so high that she had to help her to the car. She helped her into the car then went around and got into the driver's seat.

Chapter 13

When she got to her house she helped Dianna out of the car. Dianna put her arm around her shoulder. Amber put one of her arms around Dianna's waist and guided her to the door.

Amber put her key into the door, unlocked and opened it. They entered the house and Amber closed and locked the door. She guided Dianna to her bedroom.

"Where are we?" Dianna asked her.

"We are at my house boo."

"Why do I feel like this?"

"Like what boo?"

"Like my body is on fire."

"You probably need to get out of those clothes."

"You so nasty!" Dianna said giggling. They got to Amber's room and she led Dianna over to her bed and sat her down. Dianna fell back onto the bed and Amber knelt down and started removing Dianna's shoes. After getting her shoes off she went to her pants.

"I got it," Dianna told her as she stood up, undid her pants, and pulled them off. Next she took off her shirt. She tried to take her bra off but had problems with the clasps.

"Can you unhook this for me?" Amber unhooked her bra and helped her out of it. Her titties fell free, "Damn boo! You got some pretty titties."

"You think my titties are pretty?" Dianna asked her then grabbed her titties and started to squeeze them.

"Hurry up and take your panties off, I want to see your pussy."

"Why, are you going to suck it?"

"I'm going to do everything to it."

"I hope you make me cum."

"I'm going to make you cum like a waterfall." Dianna stepped out of her panties. Amber looked at her nappy bush.

"Damn! You are hairy, I could get lost in there, come here." Dianna walked over to Amber and she put her hand in between her legs. Dianna opened her legs so that Amber had better access to her pussy.

Amber cuffed her pussy. She had Dianna's pussy in the palm of her hand. She took the palm of her hand and mashed it on her pussy. She started moving it in a circular motion.

Dianna moaned, "Ummm!" Amber removed her palm, which was soaked with secretion.

She brought her palm up to her mouth and began licking it.

"Yeah I'm going to suck the shit out of your pussy!" Amber told her then began taking her clothes off.

Dianna sat back on the bed and watched Amber strip. Amber's skin color was that of butter milk. The nipples on her titties were pink. Her stomach was flat and the hair on her pussy was just as curly as the hair on her head.

Dianna noticed that her finger nails and her toe nails were painted the same color, "you ready?" Amber asked as she climbed onto the bed. Dianna scooted back to the headboard and laid her head on a pillow, "I got to start at the top" Amber told her, then crawled on top of her. She laid on top of her bringing them chest to chest.

She started kissing her in the mouth. Soon the kisses trailed down to her titties. Amber was amazed at the size of Dianna's nipples, they were as fat as a pinky finger, and stood out 1/4 of an inch when erect.

Amber descended down to Dianna's pussy. When she touched it, Dianna's body shook. Amber put her hands on the back of Dianna's thighs and pushed them back, leaving her pussy fully exposed. Dianna might have been dark, but her pussy lips were a bright pink.

Amber went to town eating her pussy. She brought Dianna to a shattering orgasm. After she made her cum, she rolled off of her and told her, "It's time for you to return the favor."

She spread her legs and pulled them back. Dianna got between her legs and played in her pussy hair. Amber's pussy hair was so long that she could twist her fingers around in it. She took two of her fingers and slightly bent them, then stuck them in Amber's pussy. While she had the two fingers inside of her she used her thumb to stimulate her clit.

"What the fuck! How are you doing that?" Amber asked.

She had never experienced that trick. To be an amateur Dianna sure had skills. When Dianna started sucking her pussy she drove her mad. She looked down and watched her eat her out. She even coached her.

"That's it boo, just like that, suck this pussy!" Amber came three times in a row and fell in lust. Dianna did not know what she had just started. After she finished eating her pussy, Amber went to her closet and pulled out a strap on dildo, and they took turns fucking each other with it. When they were all fucked out they fell asleep butt naked in each other's arms.

The next day Dianna woke up to a migraine headache. She felt strange and was not even aware of where she was at. She looked over and seen Amber sprawled out, and she started getting visions from the night before. They were coming to her in bits and pieces. She couldn't understand why she felt the way that she did.

She sat up and her movement on the bed aroused Amber. Amber rolled over and opened her eyes. She smiled at Dianna, "good morning."

"Good morning," Dianna responded groggily. Amber reached over and rubbed on Dianna's breast.

"You want a little morning loving?"

"No, I don't feel so good, I feel strange."

"Don't worry that's just the X wearing off." Confused, Dianna asked, "what do you mean X?"

"The ecstasy pill that I gave you last night."

"You never gave me no ecstasy pill. I do not use drugs."

"You were kind of stiff last night, so I slipped one into your drink to loosen you up."

"What! How could you do that. That is just wrong, I could have died."

"Dianna come on, you are overreacting. It was just a little pill that helps to loosen you up. We had a good time last night didn't we?"

"I can hardly remember anything from last night."

"Trust me we had lots of fun."

"Well, I need to be getting home."

"Okay, let me just jump into the shower right quick. Do you want to join me?"

"No that's okay," Amber got out of bed and headed to the bathroom to take a shower. Dianna sat there angry at her, for slipping her a drug. If Amber was a man, what she had done would have been considered date rape. Dianna did not know if she would be able to forgive Amber for what she had done. She just wanted to get home to take a hot shower and hoped that she would start feeling better. She got dressed and went out to the living room to wait on Amber.

Amber got out of the shower, got dressed then took Dianna home. On the drive she told her, "Di, I would never do anything to harm you. I took one myself, I just knew that you were going to feel uncomfortable being up in a straight club and I wanted to loosen you up so that you could be yourself and you did. You danced up a storm last night. We had fun last night. Please don't hold what I did against me. I swear that it will never happen again. Can you forgive me please, pretty please?" Dianna thought for a second and realized that she was right, she was nervous last night. Maybe she did need something to loosen her up. After she got over the hangover maybe she would be alright. She smiled and said, "Okay I forgive you, but please give me the heads up next time."

"Deal," Amber said feeling relieved. She really liked Dianna and wanted to go further with her. She dropped Dianna off at home and headed back to her house.

Chapter14

Deidre fell into a fit of depression. She decided to not indulge in any type of sexual behavior. She chose to concentrate on taking all of her final exams so that she could graduate. She had already been accepted into a college. Her father had started a trust fund for her when she was first born to pay her college tuition.

She could not wait to get away. She and her mother still were not speaking, and Roger was still harassing her for the truth about what happened with her and Renee. Deidre would go to school then go straight home to study. She had less than a month left to graduate and she wanted to make sure that she did.

Renee had been quiet ever since she had been released from the hospital. She stayed secluded in her room. Her mother tried to get her to go to counseling, but she kept refusing.

Roger got tired of seeing his sister walking around like a mummy. They were twins, and he could feel her pain. He decided to put an end to the madness. He went to her room and knocked on her door. He got no answer, so he tried the door knob. The door was unlocked and he opened it and stepped in.

Renee was sitting on her bed reading a magazine. Roger walked over and sat on the edge up her bed.

"Hey sis, how are you?" Renee looked up at him, "I'm okay."

"Renee, I don't know what happened, but I hate seeing you like this. Whatever it is you can't just keep holding it in. It's eating you up inside. Mom is worried about you and so am I, whatever it is it can't be that bad. You can get past it, we will support you."

"You say that now, but are you going to forgive me if I tell you the truth."

"Renee, there is nothing that you could do that I will not forgive you for. It is us over anything. If it's about you and Deidre, I have already figured that out."

"I'm so sorry Roger. I don't know how I let it happen. I have never done anything like that before. I swear I didn't mean to betray you. There is just something about her, she seduced me."

"She told me that she has been messing with girls since she was twelve."

"She told you what happened?"

"No, she actually denied it, but she did tell me that she has had sex with women before."

"Are you two still together?"

"I don't know what we are right now, and I'm not worried about her. She is going off to college in a couple of months anyway and I have to figure out what I am going to do. I don't know if I'm going to go to college or enlist in the army, I am worried about you though. I want my sister back." That brought a smile to Renee's face.

"Can I have my sister back?" he asked her.

"I have issues that I have to deal with now. I have been questioning my sexuality ever since that happened. That's why I have been so depressed. I don't know who I am anymore."

"Maybe you should take mom up on her offer to get some counseling. It might be good for you. Think about it okay?" Renee brightened up, "yeah I will."

"Can I have a hug?" Renee gave her brother a long hug. They both felt relieved of stress.

When their mother came home they all had dinner together, where they chatted about different topics. Their mother was glad to see Renee in a good mood and that she and her brother were back talking. Even though they never told her what the problem had been between them she was just glad that they had gotten past it.

Chapter 15

Deidre's graduation day came. Her father sat in the front row. Her mother refused to attend the event.

After the graduation was over, her father took her out to dinner, where they talked about her next move which was college. Deidre informed her father that she wanted to go to school to be a computer analysis. Her father told her that he supported her fully.

Ÿ

A month later, Roger enlisted into the army, Dianna moved in with Amber and Deidre was on the campus at Ohio State University.

She had a month before school would be starting. She was paired up with a white girl named Melissa in one of the school's dorm rooms.

She took a liking to Melissa, who was fun and free spirited. It was apparent that she liked the black culture from the clothes that she wore to the way she talked. Melissa had been at the school for over a year and knew her way around Columbus, Ohio. She would take Deidre around the town and to all of the hot clubs.

Melissa had all types of friends from different races and she was usually the life of the party.

Deidre and Melissa would sit up in their room and talk for hours about everything from school to boys. Melissa used to walk around the room wearing only her panties and a bra like it was normal. Deidre could not help but look at Melissa's huge titties, which had to at least be a size 40DD. Melissa was a true blond, she could tell this from the blond pussy hairs that stuck out of the sides and from on top of her panties.

One night they sat up talking about the wildest things that they had ever did. Melissa had done some of the wildest things. She admitted to having sex in public places. She admitted to stripping in a nude bar before. And being involved in a gang bang where she was the only girl. She admitted that the only thing that she hadn't did was to have sex with a woman. She told Deidre that one of her boyfriend's Billy kept asking her to have sex with him and another girl, but that she could not see herself having sex with just any girl, "It would have to be with somebody that I know," she told Deidre. She then asked her, "Have you ever been with another woman?" Deidre felt that after all that Melissa had told her that there was no need to lie.

"Yeah, I have been with women before." Melissa got excited, "You have! What is it like?"

"I can't explain it I would have to show you."

"I'm down to try anything. If I like it I like it, and if I don't, I will never do it again. You want to show me now?"

"Why not, we have nothing else to do."

"We might need this." Melissa said then reached under her mattress and pulled out a long dildo that was as thick as a man's wrist.

"Damn girl that thing fits inside of you?"

"Sure you want to see? Watch!" Melissa laid back on her bed. She spit on the head of the dildo, pulled her panties to the side and slid the dildo inside of her. She sunk it in until only the part that she held in her hand was sticking out of her.

"Damn!" Deidre said when she saw her pussy had sucked in the whole thing.

Melissa started moving the dildo in and out of her pussy. Deidre heard the sloshing sound from over on her bed. It told her that Melissa's pussy was soaking wet.

She got up off of her bed and walked over to Melissa's. She sat down on the bed and told her, "Let me do it."

"Go ahead," Melissa told her as she released her hand from the dildo. Deidre put her hand around the dildo and started to slowly fuck Melissa with it. She took two fingers from her left hand to spread Melissa pussy lips, so that she could see how her inner pussy walls clung to the dildo.

Fucking her with the dildo was arousing her. She closed Melissa's long legs together then pushed them back until her knees were touching her forehead, leaving her pussy sitting out with the dildo sticking out of it.

Deidre pulled the dildo from her pussy, and put it into her mouth. She sucked all of Melissa's juices off of it. She replaced the dildo with her mouth and started sucking Melissa's pussy.

"Hey, you go girl, that shit feels good." Melissa told her as she sat up on her elbows and watched Deidre eat her pussy. First Deidre flicked out her tongue, licking the outside of her pussy lips then she started flicking her tongue over her clit. Melissa's clit got stimulated and stood out about an inch. It was bright pink, but you could see the blood flowing inside of it.

Deidre took her forefinger and her thumb and rolled her clit between them.

"Day ... umm, do that shit then." Melissa told her. Deidre put two fingers from her other hand into her mouth and got them soaked and wet. She took them and put them to Melissa's asshole. She pushed them into her asshole and they got sucked in like a Hoover vacuum cleaner

"What the fuck!" Deidre was shocked that her asshole had just pulled her fingers into it.

"Girl, you know I'm white, we do that shit. You got to put the whole thang in me." Deidre pulled her fingers from Melissa's asshole, grabbed the dildo and put it in to the hole. She pushed it and it sank in easily.

"Girl you been damaged!" Deidre told her as she started fucking Melissa in the ass with the dildo, while she sucked her pussy. Melissa went crazy, "Here it comes, you better watch out!" Deidre did not know what she meant by that until something skeeted on her face.

She quickly pulled her face back and seen that Melissa's pussy was skeeting out cum just the way a man would.

She had never seen nothing like it before. Melissa laughed, "Yeah, I should have told you, I'm a skeeter girl.

"Yeah, you should of told me that." Deidre told her laughing herself. She wiped the cum off of her face and put into her mouth.

"So did you like it, skeeter girl?"

"Liked it, bitch I loved it! You got to teach me how to do that shit. I want to be able to return the favor."

"That's enough for one night. I can't teach you everything at once. You might try and take the pee out of the master's hand," she said laughing.

"We can at least take a shower together." Melissa stated.

"Yeah, we can do that." They got up and went and took a shower together. They washed each other up, stepped out dried each other off, got into their beds and went to sleep.

Ÿ

The next day everything was back to normal for them. It was as if nothing had happened between them. That was the first time that Deidre was able to have sex with another female and no problems came from it.

"Now that's how it should be," she said to herself.

That night they sat up and talked some more. Melissa asked her, "So are you just gay or are you bisexual?"

"I go both ways, I do not like to put a label on it."

"I feel you girl. A person should be free to do whatever they feel, especially if they are not hurting anyone. So, do you have a boyfriend and a girlfriend?"

Deidre told her all the drama that she had been going through, because of her sexuality. She told her that she and her mother were not talking and the situation that had happened with Roger and Renee.

"Are you serious you had the brother and sister? That's some player shit right there."

"It was some crazy shit, my boyfriend felt betrayed and his sister went crazy. She even tried to kill herself."

"Get the fuck out of here. What did you do to her?"

"Just a little more than what I did to you last night."

"Well, she must be a weak minded hoe. I ain't going crazy about no dick or pussy. All I worry about is getting my nut. After that I'm good."

"That's why I fuck with you Lissa. You have a free heart. You must of grew up around blacks too. You talk and act like one."

"I grew up in the suburbs. There were only a few blacks out there. One of them was my best friend. I guess some of her ways rubbed off on me. I have only been with one black guy before and that was her brother. Girl he was hung like a horse. My hand could not close around his dick. He had a fetish for fucking me in my ass too. That thing he had stretched out both of my holes. Since then I only fuck with little dick white boys, that eat pussy good." Deidre started laughing, "You is one crazy girl."

"When is you going to teach me how to suck pussy, I want to be a beast."

"I will show you a little something, something." Deidre told her as she stood up and removed her shorts and panties.

"Damn girl, you have a jungle down there!" Melissa told her as she got up off of her bed. Deidre sat on the edge of her bed and spread her legs, "Come get down on the floor between my legs."

Melissa got in front of Deidre then dropped down to her knees. Deidre took two fingers and spread her pussy lips.

"You got to take your time with it. You done had your pussy sucked and you know how you want it to be sucked. Treat mine like it's yours. Some guys be all rough, biting on your clit, scraping your pussy lips with their teeth. I'm you and you are me, treat me like you want to be treated."

Melissa put her head in between Deidre's legs and began sucking her pussy. She just went with her instincts.

She licked it, kissed it and sucked on the outside of it before she pushed her tongue inside of her.

She found that she liked the taste of pussy. The smell of Deidre's pussy turned her on. She started to lick the crevices between her pussy and thighs.

She stopped and looked up at Deidre, "How am I doing?"

"Shit you do it like a pro, I was about to cum. To be good you have to be able to eat it from the back." Deidre told her then turned onto her hands and knees. Her ass was facing the end of the bed.

Melissa rose up into a squatting position. She admired the way Deidre's pussy stuck out. Her pussy lips were meaty and juicy. Melissa took both of her thumbs and spread open Deidre's ass cheeks. She stuck her face between them and started sucking Deidre's pussy as if it was a piece of fruit. She removed one of her hands from Deidre's ass cheeks and used her fingers to fuck her pussy. Deidre's pussy quickly coated Melissa's finger with her juices.

Melissa felt like doing something silly. She put her mouth back on Deidre's pussy and tried to blow bubbles. The air bubbles felt good to Deidre. She looked back over her shoulder and said, "Girl you're stupid."

"Check this out," Melissa told her as she rose up a little more and flicked her tongue over Deidre's asshole. Deidre tightened her ass cheeks. The sensation that her tongue gave her asshole was almost unbearable. It felt like having her feet tickled.

Melissa continued messing with her asshole. She blew into it, stuck her fingers into it and licked it so much. Deidre did not know that a girl could cum without having anything stimulating her pussy. The things that Melissa did to her ass made her cum twice. After she came a second time, she fell onto her stomach then rolled onto her back. She looked at Melissa and said, "Girl you nasty."

"You liked it though didn't you?"

"Hell yeah, that shit felt good. I need to get that done more often."

"Well, let me go in here and brush my teeth." Melissa said as she stood up then headed for the bathroom.

Chapter 16

Dianna had been staying with Amber. Everything was cool at first. They would kick it and go out and have fun.

As time went on she found Amber becoming more and more possessive. She would call the house several times while she was at work and if Dianna took too long to answer the phone she would question her about what she was doing. She did not want Dianna going out by herself or hanging out with her friends.

One night they were out at a gay club, and when Amber came back from the bathroom there was a girl standing there trying to talk to Dianna. Amber went ballistic, "Bitch! Get out of my girl's face." The girl looked at her like she was crazy, "Who you calling a bitch?"

"I'm talking to you hoe!"

"Bitch! You got me fucked up!" the girl said as she advanced on her. Dianna jumped off of her bar stool and got in between them.

"Chill out Amber, It ain't that serious."

"So, you go stand up here and take up for that bitch?" Amber yelled at Dianna.

"I told you about your mouth bitch!" the girl said then swung on Amber. She caught Amber on the side of her head. Amber rushed at her, but she side stepped her and grabbed a handful of her hair. She used her hair to throw her to the floor and started pounding on her. Dianna tried to pull the girl off of Amber, but two of the girl's friends ran over and jumped in. They beat Dianna down then helped their friend stomp Amber.

The club's security had to come break it up. They escorted the girls out of the club. Amber and Dianna got into the car and headed home. They did not speak on the ride home.

When they got to the house Amber started tripping, "How you go play me?"

"What the hell are you talking about? You got us jumped for nothing."

"You shouldn't have had that bitch all up in your face. I ought to beat your ass."

"Amber you tripping. You better not put your hands on me. We will tear this bitch up!"

"Oh, you popping fly bitch?" Amber said then charged at Dianna. Dianna threw her hands up, but Amber tackled her with force, she got her on the ground and sat on top of her. She started beating her in her face. Dianna put up a fight. She grabbed her hair and pulled it. She lifted up and bit Amber in the forehead.

Amber yelled, "You bit me bitch! I'm going to kill you." Dianna pulled out strands of her hair. Amber threw wild punches which busted Dianna's nose and mouth.

Dianna bit Amber in her jaw. She locked down on it and started shaking it how a pit bull shakes a house slipper. She pulled a chunk out of Amber's cheek. Amber screamed, "Okay! Okay! Let me go!"

"Is you through?"

"Yeah, I'm through."

"I'm going to let you go. If you try something I'm going to bite your nose off." she released her lock on Amber's jaw and let her hair go.

Amber jumped up and ran to the bathroom. She looked at herself in the mirror, and seen some of her cheek hanging.

"Bitch you're crazy!" she said as she ran and grabbed her keys. She ran out of the house, jumped in her car and headed for the hospital.

Dianna packed up all of her stuff and left. She was going back to her mother's house. She was tired of dealing with Amber's mess.

Ÿ

Renee had been feeling better. She had been going out and even met a guy that she liked. They had been dating for a while. She wrote and told Roger about him.

When Roger got the letter, he was happy for his sister. He couldn't wait to go home on leave to meet the guy.

They had him doing a six month tour over in Iraq. He had seen so much killing over there he did not feel nor think the same. Every day he wondered if he would make it home alive. Sometimes he wished that he had gone to college instead of joining the service. If he had gone to college he would have needed to get a grant and he did not know if he could have qualified for one.

He crossed his fingers when his platoon sergeant told them to pack up, that they were moving out, heading into hostile territory.

Ÿ

Renee and Greg had yet to be intimate and she could tell that he was becoming frustrated. She knew that men weren't like women when it came to sex. They just had to have it. She decided that it was time to give it to him.

She called his cell phone and he answered, "Hello?"

"What are you doing?"

"Na Na what's up? I'm just sitting over my boy Bobby's house playing the PlayStation."

"I guess you busy then huh?"

"I ain't never too busy for you boo."

"Awe, that's so sweet. I been thinking, I been holding out for too long. I think it's time to give you some of this Na Na."

"Girl, don't be playing with me. You are making my shit swell up just talking like that."

"I'm serious baby, I think it's time, don't you?"

"You damn right I think it's time! I think I got blue balls or some shit."

"When is you going to be through with playing the game?"

"What game, I'm in my car driving to your house."

"Boy you silly, I guess I will see you when you get here."

"Put on something sexy for me."

"I got you," Renee told him then hung up. She went into the bathroom and took a quick shower. She then oiled her body up and put on a see through teddy.

She knew that her mother would be working overtime that day and would not be home for hours.

She sat downstairs and watched TV while she waited for Greg to get there. She heard his car when he pulled into the driveway. She went to the door and waited for him to approach it. When he got on the doorstep, she opened the door to let him in. When he stepped inside his eyes almost busted out of their sockets. He could clearly see her big, dark nipples and when he looked down he could see her hairy bush through the fabric.

Renee grabbed his hand and led him up to her room. When they got there she locked her door and slid out of her teddy. Greg's dick was trying to bust out of his pants. He quickly started stripping. He took off every piece of clothing that he had on including his socks.

He went over to Renee and grabbed her. They fell onto the bed together. He let his hands roam over every part of her body. He kissed her all over. Renee closed her eyes. She was trying to enjoy the feeling. When Greg put his mouth on her pussy, Deidre's face popped up in her head. She opened her eyes shocked, "What the fuck is wrong with me?" she said to herself. She couldn't believe after all the time that had passed how she could still have vivid memories of Deidre. She knew that she was truly messed up, if every time she had sex she seen Deidre's face.

She let Greg have his way with her. He fucked her in every position that was imaginable. He brought her too many orgasms, only it wasn't him making love to her. In her mind it was Deidre bringing her to them orgasms.

She felt bad, so she decided to give him some head. She let him cum in her mouth and swallowed his cum.

Greg laid on the bed next to her feeling fulfilled. Renee on the other hand laid there feeling like something was missing. That was her first time having sex since Deidre. She figured that after having sex a couple more times, it would bring her back to normal. Little did she know that was the furthest from the truth.

Chapter 17

School had started and Deidre was all in. College was different than high school and the work was twice as hard. To top it off she had to get an on campus job so that she could have spending money. All she had time for was school and work. The only day that she got to rest was Sunday. She would call her father on that day every week.

Even though she never talked to her mother she always inquired about her. She would also ask her father had Roger called and the answer was always no.

Because of school and work she barely saw Melissa when she was awake.

She was glad when the semester had come to an end and she got time to take a break. She and Melissa hit the clubs hard. They even attended a few concerts.

Melissa introduced Deidre to a couple of her friends that were just as wild as she was. They were Pamela and Susan. Pamela stood about 5' 10" and was very slim. She was built like the typical white girl long legs, a small ass and big titties. Susan on the other hand was built like a stallion. She stood at only 5'7", but she had a humongous ass and a set of 36DD titties.

Both girls were free spirited and down with anything as was Melissa. They loved attending hip hop clubs and interacting with the thugs.

Their favorite thing to do was to attend rave parties. There they would do everything from drinking beer straight from the keg to popping ecstasy pills.

To Deidre they were fun and exciting.

One night they were all over to Susan's house drinking and listening to music when Melissa told them, "Deidre is the one that taught me how to suck pussy."

"Well, I must tell you thanks Deidre. I never had my pussy sucked the way that Melissa did it. You taught her well." Pamela told her.

"I didn't teach her all of my tricks though."

"So you think that you could do better than she did?"

"I know that I can!"

"I would like to see that!" Susan said.

"I know what!" Melissa cut in. Deidre can suck Pam's pussy, while I suck yours Susan then we can switch."

"I don't suck pussy!" stated Susan.

"No silly, me and Deidre can switch, I will go to Pam and she will come to you."

"Now that will work. I'll never turn down having my beaver tended to." Susan said laughing.

"Should we go to the bedroom?" Pam asked.

"For what? We can do it right here!" Susan told her.

"Pam, I want you to get in the recliner chair and recline it back." Deidre told her. Pam went over and got into the chair.

"You have to take all of your clothes off first dummy."

"You did not say that," Pam said as she got up and started removing her clothes.

Deidre went into the kitchen and into Susan's refrigerator and took out a tray of ice then went back into the living room.

"What are you going to do with that?" Pam asked her.

"You will see," Deidre told her as she began breaking the ice up. Deidre started taking her clothes off.

"What are you doing?" asked Pam.

"If you are going to do something you have to do it right. I can't just go straight to your pussy. I got to work my way down to it."

She stripped naked then went over to the recliner chair. She had a piece of ice in each hand. She sat on top of Pam and rubbed the ice against both of her cheeks.

Then she trailed the ice down to her titties. She used each hand with the ice in them and rubbed all over her breast. The cold sensation made her nipples get as hard as a rock.

Deidre kept ice on one of her breast, and replaced the ice on the other breast with her mouth. Pleasure went all through Pam's body. As the ice melted, it trailed down her navel and made a puddle inside of it.

Pam started to moan. Her moaning caused Susan to look over at them. To Susan it was just fun. Melissa had her on her back, with her legs spread and up in the air eating her pussy. She didn't do any foreplay and Susan was not feeling like Pam was.

Deidre placed the ice into her mouth. She put it between her teeth, and then made a trail down to Pam's pussy.

Once she got to her pelvic area, the cool sensation started to feel good. Pam put both of her legs over the arms of the chair and laid back.

Deidre crawled down onto the floor onto her knees to give her a better angle. She used her mouth to rub the ice all over Pam's pussy.

Pam's body started to shiver. "Ooh ... Oooh! Yes! Yes!" Pam said out loud. Melissa felt like she was being out done, so she had

Susan get on her hands and knees and started licking her ass, which did have a better effect on her.

The cold ice stimulated Pam's clit and it stood straight out. Deidre felt that it was time to replace the cold sensation with a warm one. She removed the ice from her mouth, and then put a peppermint inside of it. She sucked on the peppermint which heated her mouth up. First she blew her hot breath onto Pam's clit. The heat mixing on with the cold chill sent Pam into ecstasy. Then Deidre put her mouth on her pussy. The vapors from the peppermint made Pam start cumming.

"Jeez ... I'm cumming, oh Deidre, I'm coming baby, God I'm cumming!" Pam said as her body rattled.

Deidre took a piece of ice and stuck it into Pam's asshole as she continued to suck her pussy. Pam's body went into a fit of convulsions.

"Damn, what is she doing to her?" Susan asked.

"I'm ready, let's switch? I want some of that!" Susan stated. Deidre and Melissa got up to switch positions.

When Melissa approached Pam she waved her off, "I'm done I can't take no more." Pamela tried to stand up, but her legs had no strength. She held onto the arms on the chair until the feelings came back into her legs. Then she walked as if she was bow legged to the bathroom with an ice cube still up in her ass.

Deidre did the same routine on Susan and drove Susan crazy. Deidre felt sorry for Melissa, so she called for her to come over and join her with Susan. Together they freaked Susan. Melissa sucked her breast and toes. They got Susan aroused to the point that she went against her word. Before it was all over Deidre was sitting on Susan's face and Susan was sucking the juices out of her pussy.

When it was all over it was voted unanimously that although Melissa was a good ass eater, Deidre was the better pussy eater. With that being said the girls took turns showering then sat down and watched a movie until they all fell asleep.

Chapter 18

Amber had been trying to get back with Dianna, but Dianna was not having it. She did not like violence. She did not let men hit on her, so she felt that she definitely wasn't going to let a woman beat on her.

One thing that she learned from her relationship with Amber was that having a relationship with a woman was no different than having one with a man. She even found that having one with a woman could be worst. Women are more possessive and are prone to be more jealous, and that jealousy leads to violence.

Amber stalked Dianna for over a month. Sometimes she would sit outside of Dianna's house and wait for her to come out of the house at which time she would confront her.

One day she even went to the extreme. Dianna walked out of her house heading to her car and Amber rose up from the other side of her car and scared her, "Hey Dianna!"

Dianna almost jumped out of her shoes, "Girl what is wrong with you. Why are you here?"

"I miss you and I love you."

"Well, I don't know what to tell you. I'm not fucking with your crazy ass anymore."

"I'm sorry Di, I swear I will never act like that again. Just give me another chance."

"My aunt's husband used to tell her that after he would beat her and she would always go back. My aunt is dead now, he killed her."

"I would never do that to you, I love you can't you see that?"

"All I can see is that you are crazy and I'm not going to give you a chance to kill me." Amber got mad at Dianna for rejecting her and became hostile, "Bitch! You can't just up and leave me like that. You are not going to just walk over me like that." Dianna was tired of arguing with her, so she got into her car and started it up.

As she was pulling out of the driveway her back window shattered. She looked back and there was a brick in her backseat. She threw her car in park and jumped out, "Bitch! I'm going to kill you!" she said to Amber as she went after her.

Amber was no fool. She quickly ran to her car and got in it. She started it up and drove slowly taunting Dianna yelling out of her window, "It ain't over 'til I say it's over bitch!"

"I'm going to beat your ass when I catch you. Matter of fact I'm going to press charges on you!" Dianna yelled after her.

Later that day, Dianna went to the police station where she filed a police report and requested that a restraining order be put on Amber.

She realized that she had never gone through that much drama with a man. She thought about calling Fred. She felt that she owed him an explanation after what had happened at the club.

Roger had gotten discharged from the service after serving less than a year. While his convoy was riding through hostile territory they were fired upon. A hand held rocket had hit the truck that he was riding in and his body had been riddled with shrapnel.

Roger was given a purple heart and given an honorable discharge.

Most of the shrapnel had lodged into his legs and lower back. He went through extensive rehabilitation and walked with a slight limp in his left leg.

Since he had been home he had been doing a lot of drinking. He was receiving disability and had too much time on his hand.

One night he was up in a bar. He sat at the bar nursing a drink when Fred slid onto the stool next to him, "What's up Roger?" Roger raised his head up and looked at him.

"Oh, what's up Fred?"

"I heard what happened to you over there. Are you okay man?"

"Yeah, I'm good."

"Was there a lot of killing over there?"

"Was it many people dying every day?"

"What are you going to do now that your back?"

"Shit, there isn't much that I can do with my injury and all."

"Have you heard anything from Deidre?"

"No, I haven't heard anything from that dike bitch."

"What! Deidre really is a dike? I thought that was just a rumor?"

"It's no rumor she is a bush trimmer."

"Man, what is wrong with these bitches? You know Dianna is diking now too?"

"Your girl Dianna?"

"My used to be girl Dianna. Some crazy bitch stabbed me over her at a club. I was about to kill the bitch, if Rodney hadn't stopped me."

"That shit sounds crazy. I can't figure out why all these women are becoming dikes."

"I believe it's that Jerry Springer shit. He and that hoe Ellen. Ever since his show started promoting that shit and Ellen went public, girls have just been coming out of the woodwork." Fred said.

"Then you got them activist bitches talking about we are running women into the arms of other women by abusing them. I never laid a hand on Deidre."

"I never laid a hand on Dianna either."

"I guess we will never be able to figure women out."

"I guess we won't," responded Fred as he got up from his seat.

"You be easy dawg," he said to Roger then walked off.

Roger sat there thinking. He knew that Deidre was away at college. He figured that maybe she would come home for holiday break. If she did he would go see her and see if she had gotten that shit out of her system.

He saw that his sister was back to normal. She had a steady boyfriend and all. Roger was happy for her.

Chapter19

Deidre had knocked a year of school down. She only had a year to go to receive her Associate's degree. After that she could decide if she wanted to continue on to get her Master's degree.

Her classes were starting to get harder and harder. She had an English professor that stayed on her back. It was as if she was singling her out. Her name was Mrs. Hanson and she was of German descent. She would always tell Deidre, "You could do better. You should apply yourself more." Deidre would simply respond, "I understand Mrs. Hanson."

Mrs. Hanson was in her mid-40's. She was strikingly beautiful. She had the walk of a trained model. She often wore short skirt suits to work. The boys would drool over Mrs. Hanson especially when she would bend over to help someone at their desk. Her plump ass would poke out whenever she bent over. Those who were sitting in front of the desk that she would be bent over at, would usually get a peek at her breast. Mrs. Hanson's shirts were usually low cut and if you were taller than her or were around when she was bent over, or sitting at her desk, then you were sure to get a peek at her boobs.

Mrs. Hanson seemed to be real strict and the no nonsense type. Deidre noticed that every time Mrs. Hanson decided to help her, that she always found a way to touch her. She would even bend over her allowing her breast to brush up against her. Deidre thought if she did not know any better that Mrs. Hanson was trying to come on to her.

One day Mrs. Hanson approached Deidre and told her, "I Would like for you to stay after class. I would like to show you a few things."

"Okay Mrs. Hanson," Deidre responded.

After class Mrs. Hanson got out her instructor's manual, then called Deidre up to her desk, "You can come up here Deidre your desk is too small for the both of us.

Deidre got up and went up to Mrs. Hanson's desk.

"Here you take my seat, I will stand," she told Deidre.

They started going over things in the book. After a while Mrs. Hanson came with questions that had nothing to do with school.

"So Deidre, where are you from?"

"I'm from Cleveland."

"Oh, so you're right at home."

"I wouldn't call being over three hundred miles away, being at home."

"Do you have a boyfriend that you're going home to for the holidays?"

"I don't plan on going home for the holidays."

"Oh dear why not? You have to have family and love ones that are missing you?"

"Let's just say that I don't want to have to deal with the hassle."

"Well, how about you come to my house for the holidays. I and my husband have a spare room. We would love for you to come."

"That's okay Mrs. Hanson, I'm not a charity case."

"No, no dear I would never see you as that. It is more for our benefit than yours. We have a big old house and it's just us there. We would love to have company please say yes." Deidre thought about it for a minute. She figured that she did not have anything to do over the holidays and that Melissa was probably going to spend the holidays with her boyfriend, so she said, "What the heck, I will do it." Mrs. Hanson got excited and gave Deidre a big hug and a kiss on her cheek.

Ÿ

Two weeks had passed and it was the last day of school before Christmas break.

When school let out, Mrs. Hanson drove Deidre to her dorm room so that she could get her luggage. Then they headed out to Mrs. Hanson's house, which was located out in the suburbs. Deidre was amazed at the type of houses that they were driving by. They looked like mansions, some even looked like castles.

Mrs. Hanson pulled into the driveway of a three story brick home that looked like it could house four families, yet Mrs. Hanson said that it was only her and her husband that stayed there.

The driveway of the house was about as long as a street. Mrs. Hanson pulled to a stop at the side entrance of the house and she and Deidre exited the car.

Mrs. Hanson opened the door and they stepped into the foyer. The home was beautiful inside. Mrs. Hanson led her through the kitchen and up some stairs that turned circular. Up on the second floor, Mrs. Hanson led her to a room that was almost the size of a small apartment.

"There we are dear. This will be your room. Our room is right next to yours and on the other side of our room is the bathroom. You go ahead and get your things situated. I have to get dinner started before Henry gets home." Mrs. Hanson left Deidre to unpack. She went to her room and changed out of her work clothes.

Mrs. Hanson slipped into a pair of shorts, a t-shirt that had no bra underneath it and a pair of house shoes.

She headed down to the kitchen and started cooking. She set three places at the table. She cooked some Loin chops, scallop potatoes and string beans, she also made a salad and set out the wine glasses.

She was cooking the last of the meal when Deidre came down the stairs. The aroma of the food filled her nostrils. The food smelled delicious.

Mrs. Hanson looked up, "Have a seat, I will be through in a minute." Mrs. Hanson went back to doing what she was doing, Deidre looked at Mrs. Hanson in the shirt and the shorts. She looked totally different.

She even had her hair down. Deidre took in how Mrs. Hanson still had the shape of a woman half her age, and when Mrs. Hanson would turn to face her, she could see that her titties were sitting up without the help of a bra. She started to see Mrs. Hanson in a different light.

Deidre heard the door open and close then in walked a tall man, that was strikingly handsome. His hair was dark brown except for at his temples where it was gray. He had a somewhat long chin, but besides that, Deidre thought that he could have been a model in his younger years.

He was oblivious to Deidre being there as he wrapped his arms around his wife, stuck his hand inside of her shorts and up into her pussy. He pulled his finger out and put it in his mouth, "Mmm, dinner tastes good."

"Henry, you stop it, we have company."

"Well why didn't you say anything," he turned and seen Deidre sitting there blushing.

"Why, you must be Deidre, you are just as beautiful as Helen said you were how are you?"

"I'm fine Mr. Hanson,"

"You are a guess in our house. That Mr. and Mrs. stuff has got to go out of the door. You call me Henry and call her Helen. You got that?"

"Yeah, I got it."

"Well then shall we eat." Helen took the rest of the food off of the stove and fixed their plates. They sat and ate the meal, and then Helen served some strawberry shortcake for desert. After that she filled their wine glasses and they moved into the living room.

In there they sat and talked, "So your here with us for the holidays?"

"Yes sir,"

"There you go again."

"Oh, I'm sorry, I mean Henry."

"That's better, don't you think that me and my wife are some old coots either. We are fun to be around. We do everything from streaking to skinny dipping in our pool."

"Henry, you stop that now,"

"Well it's the truth Helen. I'm not about to change because we have company. So Deidre if you so happen to see an old man walking around nude with a shriveled up penis, you pay me no mine sweetheart." Deidre just giggled. She thought that Henry was funny. She like Henry and Helen, they seemed so down to earth.

"Well Helen, we better be getting some sleep. We have to go shopping for a tree tomorrow morning."

"Oh goodness, I forgot dear. Deidre you make yourself comfortable. You can do anything that you choose to do. The entertainment system's remote is right over there on the table. You need to use the phone its right over there." she said pointing to it.

"We will see you in the morning." Helen and Henry went up the stairs.

Deidre picked up the remote and turned on the television. She turned to a movie that ended up being boring and dozed off while watching it. When she woke up the TV was fuzzy. There wasn't any programming on. She cut it off then headed up stairs. She needed to use the bathroom before she went to bed, so she headed to it. She had to pass the Hanson's bedroom to get to the bathroom.

As she walked past the room she heard some moaning. She looked and seen that the door was cracked open. She put her face in the crack of the door and seen, that Henry was fucking Helen from the back. They were facing away from her. There was a large mirror over their bed and they were facing it. All Deidre could see were Henry's back and his huge balls hanging down as he banged his wife. Deidre watched Henry's ass tighten every time he went into his wife.

The whole scene aroused Deidre. She hadn't been into voyeurism since she was a kid, but she could not take her eyes off of the old couple. It was funny to her, hearing two old white people talk during sex. "Oh, Henry you're such a tiger."

"Your vagina is so exquisite my dear. I just love pounding your pussy."

"Yes, fuck me Henry." Deidre could not believe that it was the same Mrs. Hanson in there that had all the boys terrified at school. If they could only see what she was seeing. Deidre found herself getting aroused. She cracked the door opened a little more. She leaned on the door frame stuck her hand inside of her panties and put her fingers inside of her pussy. She fucked herself with her fingers as she watched Henry fuck his wife.

Henry put his hands on his wife's shoulders as he picked up speed and started fucking her relentlessly, "Oh shit! Here it comes Helen, Oh boy!" Henry sunk into her and just held onto her hips as he shot his load in her. Unknown to Deidre, Henry had seen her in the door all along through the mirror.

Henry turned his head around and winked at Deidre.

She was embarrassed at being caught. She quickly closed the door and headed to the bathroom.

Chapter 20

The next morning they all ate breakfast together. When they finished with breakfast they went to purchase a Christmas tree.

They asked Deidre to come with them to help them pick a tree. Deidre sat in the back seat of the Mercedes and enjoyed the smell of the Italian leather.

They went to a tree farm, where Deidre helped them to pick a tree that was almost six feet tall.

"How about we do a little shopping dear," Henry told his wife. They went to the mall to purchase some gifts. They stopped in a lingerie store, where Helen selected some lingerie, "I might as well get you a few things also Deidre." she said.

"No, that's okay Helen."

"Stop it now, it is no big deal. I think this would look lovely on you. What do you think Henry?" Henry looked over and seen that Helen held a two piece lingerie set that was crotchless.

"Oh yes dear that would look beautiful on Deidre."

"There it is then, I will have them ring it up. How about we pick up a few toys darling?" asked her husband.

"Why not." Helen paid for her purchases with a platinum credit card.

Deidre thought that maybe they were going shopping for their grandkids or nieces and nephews when they mentioned getting some toys, but to her surprise they entered into a sex toy shop.

There Helen purchased all types of creams and lotions. She bought a clit ring and a hand held stimulator.

Henry had gone off by his self and returned with some beads, "How do you like these dear?"

"Oh, Henry those beads are too big to go around my neck,"

"These are not for your neck honey. These are what you call anal beads. These lovely things go inside of your spintcher. You have to get them."

"You are so naughty!" Helen said to him as she took the beads out of his hand.

She again, paid for the things with her card, and they left. Deidre thought to herself, "They are a freaky old couple."

They stopped at a nice restaurant and had a small lunch, and then they headed home. Once they got home, they set the tree up, and trimmed it. They put the decorations on it, and then cleaned up the mess that was left.

They were all worn out after all of that activity. "I say we should get a few drinks and jump into the hot tub." Henry said.

"That sounds like a good idea dear. I will get the drinks. Deidre you have to get changed to come and join us."

"I did not bring a bathing suit with me."

"Who needs a bathing suit dear? It is only us here. Just wear your panties and bra. The hot tub is on the lower level. You go get changed and meet us down there in twenty minutes.

Deidre went up to her room. She took off her clothes, leaving only her panties and bra on. She grabbed a towel and wrapped it around her upper body.

There was a tap at the door, and then the door opened. In walked Henry and to Deidre's surprise he was totally naked. What even surprised her more was the size of his penis. It hung down past the middle of his thigh and looked to be about three inches in width. She could only imagine what it looked like when it was fully erect.

"Deidre honey, are you ready to join us?" Henry asked her. Deidre could not answer. She stood in a trance looking at what hung between his legs.

"Deidre come, come now, you act like you never seen one of these before." Henry said to her as he took one of his hands and lifted his dick up.

"White men do not suppose to have penises that size." Deidre responded.

"Well my dear, I'm not what you would call the average white man. I'm what is referred to as an Italian Stallion. By the way how did you like the show last night?" Deidre felt embarrassed about being busted watching them have sex.

"I did not mean to snoop in on you two. I was just curious as to what was going on and the door was open."

"Don't sweat it, actually me and Helen are into voyeurism. Now come on we can't keep Helen waiting."

Together they walked to the lower level of the house. They walked side by side with Henry's dick swinging freely.

When they got to the lower level and entered the spa room, Helen was already in the hot tub. She was totally nude also. She had her head laid back on the edge of the hot tub.

"Here we are honey," Henry said to her.

"Well it is about time. I've given myself an orgasm with this," she pulled her hand from under the water and showed Henry the hand held stimulator that slid onto her fingers.

"You started the party without us, you naughty girl, you must pay for that."

Henry walked over to the hot tub and stood over Helen, he let his dick hang down over her face. With her head bent backwards, Helen lifted it up and took Henry's dick into her mouth.

Henry just stood over her, dick feeding her.

Deidre sat there watching the scene, mesmerized at the way Helen was sucking Henry's dick in the position that she was in. Deidre's mouth began to water. She wondered what Henry's dick tasted like. She did not have to wait long.

Henry pulled his dick from his wife's mouth and approached Deidre who was sitting on the edge of the hot tub. "Deidre my darling you must have some of this," Henry told her as his dick pointed straight at her mouth with no help. Deidre noticed that his dick had a slight curve to it. Before she took him into her mouth she looked over to Helen who said, "Go ahead dear have some." Deidre reached out with her hand and grabbed hold of Henry's dick. She then scooted closer to the edge and took him into her mouth. Her mouth felt like it was filled with a handful of walnuts. She needed the assistance of both of her hands to handle Henry's dick. While she was tending to Henry's dick, she felt her bra being unclasped. It was Helen who had undid her bra and began rubbing on her breast, "You feel so beautiful deary. Henry let me taste her."

Henry withdrew his dick from Deidre's mouth. He helped her to stand up and to remove her panties. After removing her panties he had her lay back down on the edge of the hot tub.

His wife got in between Deidre's legs. She stuck two fingers inside of Deidre's pussy then withdrew them and put them into her mouth, "Mmm, delicious dear," she said as she lowered her head in between Deidre's legs.

Henry put his dick back into Deidre's mouth and she sucked on it as if it was a pacifier.

Deidre liked the feeling that she was getting from giving and receiving pleasure at the same time. Helen really knew how to suck pussy.

She played with Henry's balls while she gave him head. The weight of his balls was so heavy that she could use them to work out her wrist.

"It is time that we switch darling. I must get into this fine specimen." Henry said.

He and Helen switched positions only she got on top of the ledge and squatted down.

"The elevator is coming down," she said as she lowered her pussy down Deidre's face.

Henry had one leg inside of the hot tub and the other on the floor beside it, as he stood between Deidre's legs. He took his arms and pushed his hands under Deidre's ass, lifted her, then pulled her to him. His dick stuck straight out, as he pulled her pussy to it. When his head was at her entrance he slowly pushed in. Deidre felt like she was a gas tank that was being filled up.

"Ah, yes ... Yes," Henry said as he sunk into her.

"So wet and so tight dear." Deidre moaned into Helen's pussy as Henry fucked her. Henry had never been with a black woman before. He had only heard about their sexuality. Just to know that he was fucking her turned him on. He found that he could not control himself. He started fucking Deidre with force. He was fucking her so hard that it was making her body shake. She could not concentrate on Helen's pussy, because of the way that he was fucking her. It felt like the hook in his dick was hitting against the side of her pussy walls.

Deidre grabbed her legs and pulled them back, even though his dick brought pain it also brought pleasure and she wanted to experience more of it.

Henry looked down and seen how Deidre's pussy had coated his dick with a thick white cream.

"That's enough of that. It's time that I mount you. Please assume the doggy position, let her up Helen."

Helen got up, so that Deidre could get up and get on her hands and knees. Henry mounted her. He put his hands on her shoulders and sunk all the way into her.

He started pounding into her again. Deidre had to grip the sides of the hot tub for support.

Helen felt left out, so she positioned herself on her back up under Henry and began to suck his balls.

Henry removed his hands from Deidre's shoulders and placed them on the small of her back. Deidre coaxed him on as he fucked her, "You a beast Henry, do that shit then. Give me that Italian dick." Those words sent Henry over the edge. Helen felt his body began to tense up and took one of her hands and put it on the base of Henry's dick. She jacked Henry's dick as he slammed into Deidre.

"Fill her up!" she said as he began blasting off into Deidre. Helen helped him along. She milked him like a cow. She made sure that all of his cum went inside of Deidre.

That night was only the beginning. For two weeks they had sex with each other. They even played naked twister and went skinny dipping in their outside heated pool in the dead of winter. Henry and Helen both vied for a long time with Deidre.

Helen came into Deidre's room one night and had Deidre use the anal balls on her. They sixty nined with each other, and munched on each other's pussy as if they were fresh pieces of fruit.

Early Christmas morning Henry entered into Deidre's room wearing nothing but a Santa's hat and bearing two gifts.

"Ho … Ho … Ho … Merry Christmas Deidre darling!" Henry said to her waking her up out of her sleep.

Deidre rolled over and sat up. Henry was standing at the edge of her bed. He had a red ribbon tied around his dick in a bow. He also had a small wrapped gift in his hand. "Take this one first dear." he said handing Deidre the wrapped gift. She opened it up and found a five thousand dollar tennis bracelet.

"That is a gift from me and Helen, a token of our appreciation. Go ahead and put it on." Deidre put the diamond bracelet onto her wrist.

"And now it's time to open your other gift." he told her as he stood before her with his dick sticking out, curved to the left at the end.

Deidre untied the bow from his dick and put his dick in her mouth. She loved the way Henry's dick would pulsate inside of her mouth. She closed her eyes and made love to his dick.

"Ah, that's it my love," Henry told her as he cuffed the back of her head.

When he felt that he was getting to the edge, he had Deidre stop, "Please lay on your side." Deidre laid on her side on the bed and Henry got into the bed behind her.

"Please pull your legs up and bend them." Deidre bent her legs at the knees and drew them up to her chest. Henry used one hand to separate Deidre's ass cheeks and used the other one to guide his dick into her. He sunk into her and whispered into her ear, "Deidre my dear, I must tell you that you are the first black woman that I have ever had sex with, I must tell you that you are a very fine specimen. You are truly beautiful. Your pussy is so tender and wet. Sticking my dick inside of you is like taking a dip into the fountain of youth." Deidre put an arch into her back to toot her ass out more to receive all that Henry could give.

Henry wrapped his arms around Deidre's upper body and fucked her with passion. He kept talking to her which heightened her arousal and led her to three orgasms.

After Henry was done with her, he went back to his bedroom to tend to his wife, who eagerly sucked Deidre's juices off of him.

At the end of the holiday break they took Deidre and bought her lavish gifts, including a diamond clit ring.

Deidre was sad when it came time to leave. Helen and Henry made her promise not to be a stranger. They both drove her back to her dorm and dropped her off. When she got out of the car, before she entered the building she waved at them and they waved back.

Ÿ

When Deidre entered her room, Melissa was sitting up in her bed. When she seen Deidre enter the room, her face lit up.

She jumped up off of her bed and ran over to give Deidre a hug.

"Damn girl let me put my bags down." Deidre told her laughing.

"Bitch! I missed you."

"I missed your crazy ass too."

"Okay, get settled in so you can tell me everything. I know that something had to happen."

"Alright let me unpack." Deidre unpacked and put up her clothing and her gifts that Henry and Helen had bought her. Afterwards she went and flopped down onto Melissa's bed.

"So bitch, tell me the story." Melissa said to her.

"I had a good time with my professor and her husband."

"You had sex with your professor are you crazy! You could get expelled."

"Whose going to tell? No one knows but you,"

"Isn't your professor old?"

"She is in her mid-40's, but she has a sex drive like a 20 year old. She also has a lovely body and knows how to eat pussy. Her husband, he is Italian and is hung like a horse. My pussy is still sore, see this," Deidre said as she showed off the bracelet.

"Bitch, is that real?"

"Real as your titties bitch!"

"They gave you that?"

"They gave me this and a diamond clit ring."

"You go girl, but you know that I'm mad at you?"

"Mad at me for what?"

"You went and had sex with those people, but you couldn't have sex with me and Billy."

"Hoe, don't you try that. You have never once mentioned anything about me having sex with you and Billy. You only mentioned that Billy wanted to have sex with you and another woman. You never asked me, so don't be tripping. If you want me to have a three way with you and little dick Billy, I will do it. Now I need to get me some sleep."

Ÿ

School started back and Deidre was all in. Things were going well until she received a call from her mother.

She was surprised when Melissa told her that her mother was on the phone. Before she grabbed the phone she knew that something had to be wrong for her mother to be calling her.

She got on the phone and her mother told her that her father had been in a car accident and was hurt pretty bad and that she needed to come home.

The next day Deidre went to her school counselor and told him the situation. He agreed to let Deidre do her school work online until she got back from her family emergency. The next day Deidre was on a Greyhound heading to Cleveland, Ohio.

Chapter 21

Renee had secretly started attending gay bars. Sex with her boyfriend just was not cutting it for her. She had a couple one night stands with woman, but neither time did she get the feeling that she had experienced with Deidre. "What is it? What is wrong with me?" she asked herself.

She found that she couldn't be pleased by neither a man nor a woman.

"Deidre must have put a curse on me," she thought to herself.

She continued to have sex with her boyfriend just as a routine. Most of the times she faked having orgasms.

Ÿ

Dianna called up Fred and they met for drinks. Dianna told him that she apologized for not being truthful with him. She told him that she still loved him and that maybe they could try to work things out.

"Di, you know that I care about you. What you did to me really hurt me. It is not the fact about you wanting to be with a woman. It is about you not being honest with me."

"Fred, I understand what you are saying, but I was confused. These are feelings that I have been battling with since I was a kid. I just wanted to try to find myself."

"So do you know what you want now? I mean do you want to be with a man or a woman? We could do it together and that way there won't be any betrayal involved."

"So, what you're saying is we can have an open relationship?"

"No, it's not an open relationship, because everything that we do will be done together not apart."

"And how would we go about picking the girls?"

"We will take turns, sometimes you will pick them and sometimes I will." Fred thought about it. That was like having his cake and eating it too.

"When are we going to start?"

"We can start right now. All we have to do is go to a gay bar and I can pick a girl that is interested in having a threesome with us."

"Shit! I ain't stepping foot in no gay bar. I don't want nobody thinking that I'm gay."

"We can go to a girl's gay bar. Men be in there also."

"That will work. I will follow you in my car." They headed out of the bar and got into their cars and Dianna led the way to the Girl's gay bar.

They got to the bar and went in. They took a seat at a table and started looking over the club, trying to find a girl that sparked both of their interest and who would possibly be interested in having a threesome with them.

"What about her?" Dianna asked pointing to a light skinned, short girl that had a Halle Barry bob.

"She alright, but she is kind of small." They kept looking, "What about her over there?" asked Fred pointing out a Hershey's chocolate complexion woman, who was thick as Buffy the body.

"That's all you care about is a woman's body. You would fuck a headless woman as long as she has a body." Dianna said laughing.

"Yeah whatever, you got a body."

"Yeah, but I look good too."

"Okay Beyoncé, go get her then." Dianna sashayed over to the dark skinned girl and introduced herself.

"Hi my name is Dianna."

"Hi Dianna, my name is Marva."

"I might as well get to the point Marva. I'm here with my boyfriend and we are trying to find someone that would be interested in having a three way with us."

"What made you pick me and how do you know that I mess with men?"

"Actually, it was him that picked you. I'm just the pitch person. And as far as you messing with men, I didn't know if you did or not. I'm just shooting my shot."

"You say he picked me. What you don't find me attractive?" Dianna looked her up and down, "I find you very attractive."

"And having sex with you and your boyfriend won't cause any problems, because I'm not trying to get caught up in no drama."

"No, there won't be any drama. We are all consenting adults."

"I will tell you what, tonight is your lucky night. It's not about your boyfriend though. I'm going to do it just because I want to be with you. And you tell him that I ain't sucking his dick. I don't play that shit."

"Okay, I will tell him. Come on over with me so that I can introduce the two of you and we can go make this happen."

"Hold up for a minute," Marva called out to the bartender, "Give me another double." The bartender brought her another double of Hennessy and she downed it then said, "Okay, let's go."

She followed Dianna over to Fred and Dianna introduced them, "Fred this is Marva, Marva this is Fred." Fred reached out and shook Marva's hand.

"So where are we going?" Marva asked.

"I suggest that we get a hotel room. I'm sure that Fred doesn't mind paying for it," Dianna said. Fred, who was hype said, "I got it."

"If you don't have any condoms, I suggest that you stop off somewhere and get some. Matter of fact, I might need some more to drink." Marva advised him.

"Don't worry I got you,"

"So do you want me to follow in my car?"

"Actually we are driving in separate cars," Dianna told her.

"So we are about to be a caravan on the way to do the nasty." Marva said laughing.

They all went out and got into their cars. Fred was the lead car. First he stopped at a gas station and bought a pack of rubbers. He then headed to an after hour spot where he purchased a bottle of Remy.

They headed to the Holiday Inn where Fred got them a hundred dollar a night room. They headed up on the elevator to the 5th floor, where their room was located. When they got to their room they got comfortable.

Fred cracked the bottle of Remy and they all took turns drinking out of the bottle.

When the bottle was almost empty, Marva stood up and went over to the TV. She put it on a music station and started dancing. She started stripping as she danced. Dianna decided to join her. She got up and started dancing also. She approached Marva and they started helping each other to strip out of their clothes.

Fred just laid back on the bed and watched the show. Once they were down to their panties and bra, Dianna got behind Marva. Marva was winding her hips, and Dianna was grinding her pelvic area on her ass.

Marva reached behind her and started rubbing on Dianna's face. Dianna in return stuck her hand down into Marva's panties and started playing with her pussy. Marva leaned her head back into Dianna's chest, and spread her legs open. Dianna put three fingers inside off her and started fucking her with them. Fred's dick got hard as a brick from watching the girls.

Soon the girls stopped and slid, out of their panties and bra. They went over to the bed and crawled onto it.

Marva laid on her back and spread her legs open. Dianna got in between her legs and started sucking her pussy.

Fred had, had enough. He stripped out of his clothes and crawled onto the bed behind Dianna, who had her ass sticking up in the air as she ate Marva's pussy.

Fred entered her and began fucking her doggy style.

Dianna rocked back and forth on her knees meeting Fred's thrust as she ate Marva's pussy.

Marva was real vocal. "Suck it, oh! ... Oh suck it!" she came leaving thick cum on the top of Dianna's lips.

They all switched positions. Dianna got into the doggy style position in front of Marva,   who also got into the doggy style position. Marva ate Dianna from the back, while Fred fucked her from the back.

To Fred Marva's pussy was super-hot and wet. He held her ass cheeks apart as he watched his dick go in and out of her. She had some fat pussy lips and they clung to his dick.

"Get this pussy! Tear it up!" she said to Fred in between eating Dianna's pussy.

Fred could not believe that he was in a hotel fucking two women. He was living every man's dream. He knew that he had to take advantage of that. He had them get doggy style side by side with their asses facing the end of the bed. He stood at the end of the bed and went back and forth fucking them. He just enjoyed the pleasure that he was getting from watching his dick go in and out each of the girl's pussies.

He knew that he would always have Dianna, so he wanted to leave an impression on Marva. He had her lay on her back, and he had her close her legs and pulls them back to her chest. He kept his feet on the floor and leaned over her using his hands to support him on the bed. He started pounding Marva with force.

Marva wasn't even too much up on fucking with men. She only did it about twice a year, but she had to admit to herself that Fred was fucking the shit out of her. The way that he was fucking her was the reason why she hadn't totally given up on men. She even thought about sucking his dick, the way that he was making her feel.

Dianna felt a pang of jealousy, when she seen the look that Fred had on his face as he was fucking Marva. He had a look of intensity in his eyes that she had never seen before while he was fucking her. To her it seemed as if he was possessed. And the loud noises that Marva was making weren't making it any better for her. She silently hoped to herself that she had not created a monster.

When Fred got through with Marva, his whole body was soaking wet. He knew that he had put it on her. His chest stung from the sweat getting into the scratches that she left on it.

He wondered to himself, "How can a bitch leave this dick for some pussy." He started striking poses in front of the girls, flexing his muscles.

They showered and got dressed. Marva and Dianna exchanged numbers, only the next time that they would meet up, Dianna was going to make sure that Fred wasn't there.

Chapter 22

The bus arrived in Cleveland down at the terminal. Deidre got off of the bus and found her mother standing there. She   had come to pick her up. They left out of the station and got into her mother's car.

Her mother drove in silence. She did not even say hi or ask Deidre how she was doing.

Deidre asked her mother, "How is he?"

"He is in bad shape. They do not know if they are going to have to amputate his leg or not." The news deeply affected Deidre. Her father was her rock. He was a good man and she could not understand how God could let her father be put in the position that he was in.

They rode the rest of the way to the hospital in silence. They got to the hospital and Deidre's mother requested to see the doctor. The doctor came out into the waiting room and called for Deidre's mother to follow him. Deidre trailed behind her mother as she followed the doctor down the hall and into an office.

Once inside of the office the doctor told them to have a seat, then he began explaining the situation.

"Mrs. Ford your husband has a blood clot that has formed in his right leg, below the knee. There has been too much damage done to the leg and if the clot is not quickly tended to, it could travel up to his heart, which could become fatal. In my professional opinion your husband needs to have his leg amputated as soon as possible."

"So, you're saying that the leg cannot be saved?"

"There is too much destruction of the bone and cartilage. The leg would not be of any use to him even if it could be saved. The longer that the leg stays attached the greater the risk becomes that he will not make it. I have the necessary paperwork for you to sign right here that would give us permission to remove the leg." Deidre just sat there with tears silently running down her face as she listened to the doctor advising her mother about her father's situation. As she cried she started to realize that having a father with only one leg was better than not having a father at all.

Her mother signed the authorization papers for the doctor, and he told them that her father would be prepped for surgery immediately.

Deidre's mother asked him, "So how long will the surgery take."

"It can take anywhere from three to six hours depending on the amount of work that we have to do."

"So, I won't be able to see him until tomorrow then?"

"He should be set up in a recovery room by tomorrow evening."

"Okay, I will return then. I have to go home and get some rest. I have to be at work in the morning." Deidre could not believe her ears, there it was her father was lying up in the hospital about to lose a leg and she was worried about getting some sleep and going to work. Deidre was starting to hate her mother.

"Doc would it be okay if I stayed up here, until he comes out of surgery, I just want to stay updated on his status and to be on hand in case you need any more information regarding him." Deidre asked him.

"Sure you can stay, and me or one of the other doctors will keep you updated." Deidre turned to her mother, "I'm going to stay up here."

"Do whatever suits you," her mother told her as she turned and left.

Deidre took a seat in the waiting room. While she sat there she did a lot of thinking. She started to wonder what Roger was doing, and how did Dianna make out on her search. After hours of sitting in the waiting room doing nothing, she decided to give Roger a call.

She got up and headed over to the phones. She put a quarter in, then called Roger's house. A female answered the phone, "Hello?"

"May I speak to Roger please?"

"A shiver went through Renee's body. She knew whose voice it was on the other end of the phone. It was a voice that instantly got her pussy wet.

"Is this Deidre?"

"Yes this is she, who is this, Renee?"

"Yeah, this me, where are you at?"

"I'm at the hospital. My father has been hurt and I'm at the hospital with him."

"So, you are up here?"

"Yes, that's why I am calling to see if Roger is there."

"He is here hold on for a minute," she told Deidre then she yelled upstairs, "Roger picks up the phone." Roger picked up the phone and said, "I got it Renee." Renee put the receiver down so that they would think that she had hung up, but she then quietly picked it back up and listened to their conversation.

"How are you Roger?"

"Deidre?"

"Yes, this is Deidre."

"Where are you?"

"I'm up here at Metro Hospital."

"The Metro hospital that is on the west side of town?"

"That's it."

"And what are you doing up there?"

"My father has been in a bad accident and I had to come back to see about him."

"How long are you going to be up here?"

"I truly do not know as of right now. He is in pretty bad shape and I will not be leaving until I am for sure that he is alright. Actually I'm not leaving this hospital until I know that he is okay. I called to see if you could come up here and sit with me. Maybe we could catch up on old times."

"Sure I will come up there. Just let me get dressed and I'm on my way."

"Okay, I will be standing outside in the parking lot. It's too hot and stuffy in here."

"Okay, give me about a half an hour and I will be there." Roger told her and hung up. Renee hung up also. She sat there thinking, "She is back, and I wonder how I can see her without causing any problems." She did not have an answer right then, but she knew that she wasn't going to let Deidre leave without seeing her.

Deidre walked outside and enjoyed the cool breeze.

She looked up at the skyline, which was becoming darker by the minute.

"Is this what life is all about. Is it about facing one obstacle after another." she said to herself.

She walked over and sat down on a guardrail.

Twenty minutes later she saw some headlights turn into the parking lot. She stood up, so that she could see who it was and they could see her also. Roger seen Deidre stand up and pulled over to her. "Get in," he told her.

"I'm not leaving!"

"I know I'm just going to pull into a parking space, so that we can sit and talk." Deidre got into the car and Roger drove around the lot until he found a place to park. He pulled into the spot, cut off his headlights and killed the engine.

"They sat there looking at each other for a few minutes, and then Roger broke the awkward silence, "You look good."

"Thanks, you're looking good yourself."

"I may look good but I don't feel good."

"I heard that you got hurt over there in the war."

"That hurt was nothing compared to the type of hurt that you caused me with my sister Deidre! How could you?"

"Are we still on that, I thought we came to an understanding on that."

"No, you came to an understanding. You decided to keep lying to me, but my sister ended up fessing up. She is back to normal and our relationship is back to normal."

"I'm glad to hear that Roger. I never in no way wanted to come between you and your sister."

"You honestly did not think that you having sex with my sister wouldn't cause problems between us?"

"Truthfully, what happened between us wasn't planned. It was something that just happened and there wasn't any thought put into anything including the consequences behind our actions. I do owe you an apology, and I hope that you accept it."

"I been forgave you Deidre. I had wanted to talk to you for quite some time. I just did not know how to contact you."

"Maybe, while I'm up here we can try to work things out."

"We can do that."

"I will be up here until my father comes out of surgery. Can you come back up here and check on me tomorrow?"

"You are going to stay up here overnight?"

"Yeah, my mother had more important things to do, so I decided to stay up here."

"How is he?"

"They are about to amputate his leg."

"That is so messed up. Listen how about I go and grab us a bite to eat and come back and sit up here with you?"

"You would do that?"

"Of course I would. You go on back into the waiting room in case the doctor comes looking for you. I will go and grab us a bite to eat and be right back." Deidre reached over and gave him a kiss and a hug before she got out of the car and headed back into the hospital.

Roger drove off. He went and got them some Chinese food. When he got back to the hospital he went into his trunk and pulled out his starter jacket.

He went into the hospital and found Deidre, who had saved him a seat right next to her.

He passed her some shrimp fried rice and a soft drink. After they finished eating, Roger threw away their trash. He sat back down and put his coat over the both of them. He put his arm around Deidre and she laid her head on his shoulder. Together they fell asleep under his jacket.

The doctor woke them up nine o'clock the next morning, "Ms. Ford, your father is out of surgery and is in the recovery room. The operation was a success. With today's technology, your father will be just as active as he was before the accident."

"Can I see him?"

"Sure, he is in room 323. He is still a little out of it, but he will be able to understand you."

"Okay, thank you doctor." Deidre told him then turned and headed for the elevators with Roger following her.

They caught the elevator up to the third floor and went to her father's room. When they entered Deidre wanted to cry. Her father had tubes sticking out of him from everywhere. There was also some contraption that had his leg that had been amputated slightly raised up in the air. He also had a tube that was going up into his nose. To Deidre it looked as if he was dead.

She approached him and grabbed his hand. To her surprise, he squeezed her hand and opened his eyes. He looked at her and to her it looked as if he was smiling at her.

"I love you daddy," she told him. He squeezed her hand tighter letting her know that he understood her.

A nurse came into the room, to check the machines that he was connected to. She wrote some numbers down off of the machines then left the room.

Roger had always seen Deidre's father as the driving force behind her. He was a very strong man and he hated to see him reduced to the capacity that he was in.

Deidre sat at the side of her father's bed and Roger stood there next to her with his arm around her.

At twelve noon the doctor came into the room and told Deidre that they needed to leave the room, while they tended to her father. He advised her that she should go home and get some sleep. He told her that her father would be okay.

"Come on, I will take you home and bring you back when you are ready." Roger told her.

"Daddy are you going to be alright?" Deidre asked her father. He squeezed her hand again and she took that as a yes.

"I will be back, you just hang in there." she told her father. She turned to Roger, "Okay, come on." They left the hospital, got into Roger's car and headed to her house.

Chapter 23

They arrived at Deidre's home and went up to her room. Deidre flopped down on her bed, "I missed my bed so much!" she said.

"You missed it more than you missed me?"

"No silly,"

"Show me then,"

"I haven't showered yet, at least let me take a shower."

"How about I take one with you?"

"That sounds nice," together they went into the bathroom and hopped into the shower. Deidre stood under the hard, hot jet spray, letting the hot water sooth her tension.

Roger grabbed a washcloth and some soap off of the rack. He soaped the washcloth up and began lathering up Deidre. He reached around her while he stood behind her and washed the front part of her body. He started at her neck, and then worked his way down to her titties. He took his time washing her titties. He made sure that he washed them thoroughly, lifting each one up and cleaning under them.

When he got down to her pussy, she put one leg up on the side of the tub, and he washed between her legs. One of his fingers slipped into Deidre's pussy, and it sent a tingle through her body.

"I have missed you so much Roger." she said to him.

"Damn I love you Deidre!" he said to her as he nibbled on her ear.

He finished washing Deidre and she decided to return the favor. She took a rag, soaped it up and began washing Roger. She scrubbed his chest, which was hairy. She played with the suds on his chest. She washed his stomach then went lower. Roger put his leg up also, allowing her to get between his legs and wash his balls.

Deidre dropped down to her knees and watched as she washed his dick and balls. She tended to him like a mother does to her child.

She used her hands to hold his dick up so that the shower jet could rinse it off. When his dick and balls were free of soap she took him into her mouth. Getting his dick sucked under running hot water felt good to Roger. He put his hands on the sides of her shoulders to hold himself up. The head that Deidre was giving him was making him weak at the knees. He had not been inside of Deidre in almost two years. He wanted to feel his dick inside of her. He pulled her up and turned her around. He had her bent over at the waist. She put her hands on her knees as Roger entered her from the back.

Deidre had too much tension and frustration built up inside of her. She felt that she needed a good fucking to relieve some of it.

"Fuck me Roger, I need you to fuck me." Roger started fucking Deidre with so much force that she had to take her arms off of her knees and put them on the wall for support.

Roger got so caught up that, he lifted Deidre's legs off of the floor and held them at his sides as he fucked her. Deidre was laying horizontal in the air trying to keep her hands from sliding down the wet wall as he pounded her. Her titties hung down and shook freely. She wrapped her legs around his waist for extra support. That position was awkward and prevented him from getting a good thrust. He slid the shower curtain open and stepped out. He leaned back to keep Deidre's body parallel. When he got out of the shower he bent forward allowing Deidre to put her hands onto the floor, then he dropped down to his knees. He let go of Deidre's legs and she assumed the doggy style position. Deidre put her hands on the toilet for support, and Roger got onto his knees and started pounding her again.

"That's it Roger, that's what I need baby, fuck this pussy!"

"This my pussy you hear me, do you hear me!"

"Yes! Oh … Yes!"

"It will always belong to me. Can't no bitch or man claim this pussy but me." He bent over Deidre, put his arms up under her and cupped her breast. He raised his right leg up so that the foot was flat on the floor. He was fucking Deidre as if they were wild animals out in the forest, and she was loving it.

"Fuck! … Fuck … Fuck … I'm cumming Roger, I'm cumming," Roger slammed into her a couple more times before he shot his load. When he was through nutting, he let go of her and sat back on the floor, trying to catch his breath.

Deidre collapsed onto the floor. She laid there breathing hard. She looked at Roger, "You're still a beast. I hope that you got all your frustration at me out. I don't know if I can take being fucked like that again." Roger sat there on the floor smiling. They were both sweating all over again from the sex and the hot shower that was still running. They jumped back into the shower again. After they cleaned themselves for a second time they got dressed.

Deidre made them some sandwiches and they headed back to the hospital.

When they got there, Deidre's mother was in the room. Her father was awake and they were talking. Her father looked up when she walked into the room. A smile came across his face.

"Hey daddy?" she said as she approached him. She wanted to give him a hug, but didn't want to injure him further, so she just gave him a kiss on the cheek. Her father asked her in a low voice, "How is my baby girl doing?"

"I'm alright daddy, it's you that I am worried about."

"Don't worry about me, I will be okay."

"Don't you lie to her like that Earl," Deidre's mother told him.

"Deidre you are going to need to come home to help out with your father. I'm not going to be able to work and take care of him all by myself! Your brother has moved two states over.   I   am going to need some help."

"I have to finish school. I only have one semester left."

"You're going to choose school over your father."

"Carolynn you stop that! Stop trying to make my baby feel guilty. She needs to finish school, so that she can do something with her life. We can get a nurse to help out a couple days a week."

"And where is the money going to come from. The insurance is not going to cover it. Your medical bills aren't going to do nothing but keep climbing with all of the therapy that you are going to have to go through. A prosthetic leg is going to cost a fortune, need I go on?"

"Mom, I will go back to school until midterms, then I will transfer my classes up here to Cleveland State and I will help out with daddy. How does that sound?"

"And when is your midterms?"

"I have midterms in less than three months."

"I guess I could manage until then."

"Deidre could you and Roger step out of the room for a minute? I need to speak to your mother alone for a moment." Deidre and Roger left out of the room. Deidre's father turned to her mother, "Carolynn, it's time that you put that nonsense to an end. If she is going to put her life on hold to come back and see after me, you are not going to make her life a living hell. I would rather be put into a home before I sit around and watch my daughter be miserable. So, I'm telling you now, you accept our daughter for who she is, do not hold what she is against her. I'm begging you to do that for me, can you?" Deidre's mother sat there with tears falling from her eyes. She realized that she had been treating her daughter coldheartedly. She did not understand how she could treat someone that came from her womb so bad. She felt that she was still a woman of the Bible and did not want to go against its words. How could she accept her daughter if the things that she did went against the things that she was taught to believe in.

She knew that she would have to find a way for the sake of saving her family.

"You have my word that I will try my best."

"Trying is not good enough for me Carolynn, I need assurance."

"Okay … Okay … Earl, you have my word."

"Call my baby back in here." Deidre's mother went and called her back into the room.

She and Roger stepped back into the room. Deidre you go back down there and do whatever you have to do when you come back we will get you a car for transportation. My insurance is going to replace my car and I won't be driving anymore, so you can have it. I still want you to pursue your dream of being a computer analyst. Also I want you and your mother to work on the issues that you have. I may not be so lucky next time. Both of you are my girls and we are family and I need us to start acting like one. Now go on home and get some sleep. This medicine has me tired and I want to go to sleep." Deidre and her mother both gave her father a hug then they left.

Downstairs Deidre told her mother, "I will be there later on. Me and Roger are about to go and have a few drinks." Her mother did not have a problem with that. She hoped that Deidre had given up her alternative lifestyle.

"Okay I will see you when you get in."

Roger took Deidre to a sports bar. They sat at the bar eating wing dings and sipping on Coronas.

Dianna and Fred just so happened to be in the same bar. They were seated at a table. Dianna had went to use the restroom, and on her way she had to walk past Roger and Deidre. She had to do a double take. She could not believe it. She went around the corner and kept peeking back around it.

"That is her," she said to herself. She went ahead and used the restroom and on the way back she stopped where Deidre was sitting.

"Hey Deidre!" she said smiling. Deidre turned around on her stool, "What's up Dianna?"

"Nothing much, just up here with Fred watching the game." The last time that Deidre had seen Dianna she said that she had left Fred and was on a search to find out about her sexuality. She wondered what had happened, since she was back with Fred.

Roger cut in, "Fred is up here?"

"Yeah, he is over by the pool tables."

"I'm going to go and holla at him right quick. I will be back Deidre."

"Okay," Roger walked off and Dianna asked, "So when did you get back?"

"I got back yesterday."

"And how long are you back for?"

"I'm leaving in a day or two, but I will be back permanently in three months."

"So, are you and Roger back together?"

"I don't know what we are right now, what about you and Fred?"

"I created a monster, I thought that we could be together and share women together. That's all he looks for now are threesomes, and most times it really be a twosome because he hardly pays me any attention. I'm starting to wish I had never gotten back with him."

"Yeah, sometimes things do not go as planned. They can backfire on you."

"Has Roger accepted you for who you are?"

"Honestly we haven't talked about it."

"What happen to your quest that you went on about having a relationship with a woman?"

"It turned out horrible. Women are just as crazy as men. The bitch even stalked me." Deidre sat there laughing.

"Deidre, I would really like to spend some time with you before you go."

"I don't know if I will have time, but if I do I will give you a call."

"Is that a promise?"

"I guess you could call it that."

"Okay then, I hope to hear from you," Dianna told her as she headed back to her seat. Roger was playing a game of pool with Fred. They were both in good spirits.

"So when did you get back with Dianna?" Roger asked Fred.

"It's been a couple of months now, and it has been lovely. I see you're back with Deidre?"

"Yeah it seems that way. I guess they are tired of carpet munching. How did you get Dianna to give up sucking pussy?"

"I didn't, I just had her include me."

"Include you how?"

"Come on Roger, I know that you are not slow. We have sex with other girls together. I have been getting so many different types of pussy, it is like I have died and went to heaven."

"Sounds like fun?"

"It is, having two girls fighting over sucking your dick. Fucking two pussies as they lay side by side, there is nothing like it. So Deidre gave up her craving for the other side of the tracks huh?"

"You know, I haven't even talked to her about that. I just assumed that she was over it, being that she called me up."

"Do not go by that. Just because she is giving you some pussy does not mean that she gave up eating it herself. You better reach a clear understanding with her, before you end up getting a surprise that you don't want."

"Yeah, I guess you are right. You be easy man." Roger sat the pool stick down on the table and headed back over to Deidre.

He ordered a fresh Corona and sat on his stool. He looked at Deidre for a moment then said, "I might as well get this off of my chest. Where do we stand Deidre. What lies in our future?"

"I cannot answer that. Only time can tell us that."

"Answer this then, do you still have sex with women?"

"Yes I do,"

"What kind of relationship can we have if you are still confused about your sexuality?"

"Roger, I'm not confused about my sexuality. I have come to terms with it. I like both sexes that's all to it. Look we are moving too fast anyway, let's talk about these things when I come back. Right now I have to worry about my father and school. We can see what happens when I come back from school. Let's just enjoy each other for now. Can we do that?"

"Yeah, we can do that."

"Can we stay at your house tonight?"

"Sure we can," They left the bar and headed to Roger's house. When they got there everyone was asleep. They headed up to Roger's room, where they slipped out of their clothes and got into the bed.

While they were having sex, Renee laid up in her bed in the dark and just imagined what they were in there doing. She was not asleep when they came into the house. She had heard Roger's car when it pulled into the driveway, and she had went to her window. She had eased her curtain back and seen Roger and Deidre get out of the car. For a minute she thought about eavesdropping on them again, but she did not want to bring anymore agony upon herself.

Chapter 24

The next day, Roger took Deidre home so that she could shower and change clothes. She fixed them some breakfast, and after they ate they headed back up to the hospital to see Deidre's father.

The nurse told them that they were going to have to wait until the doctor finished changing his dressing.

"So when are you leaving?" Roger asked her.

"I will probably go back tomorrow. I have to get my work done if I want to be able to transfer my credits up here."

"Maybe I can drive down there on the weekends sometimes."

"That would be great. There are a lot of things that we can do down there. We could even take a trip to Kings Island."

"You just call and let me know when it is okay to come and I am there."

The nurse came and told them, "You can go in and see him now."

"Thank you," replied Deidre, then her and Roger entered the room. Her father had his bed lifted up in the back almost putting him in a sitting position.

"How are you today daddy?"

"I'm okay sweetheart, just a little drunk off of all of those drugs that they keep pumping into me."

"Do you know how long you will be in here?"

"The doctor told me that I will be in here, for at least six to eight weeks. I will probably just be getting home when you're on your way back."

"I was thinking about going back tomorrow, so that I could get ahead on my work and probably be able to come home earlier. If you need me to, I will stay a little while longer."

"No … No … You go ahead. I will be alright. I'm just going to worry your mother to death. Give her something else to complain about." he said laughing.

He looked over to Roger, "How are you boy?"

"I'm fine Mr. Ford."

"I don't know the situation with you and my baby girl. But whatever it is you make sure that you keep her happy, do you hear me?"

"Yes, I hear you Mr. Ford and you do not have anything to worry about."

"Well you kids go on. I don't need nobody sitting up here having pity for me. Let me rest in peace. Deidre you just call me from time to time and let me know that you are okay."

"I will daddy," Deidre told him as she went over to him and gave him a kiss and a hug.

"I love you daddy."

"I love you too baby girl." Deidre and Roger left. Roger asked her, "Where to now?"

"I want to go home and get me some rest. You can come and take me to the bus station in the morning if you want."

"I will do that. What time does your bus leave?"

"I'm going to have to call down to the station, when I find out what time the bus is leaving I will call and tell you."

Roger dropped Deidre off at home. She was exhausted and went up to her room and crashed out.

"She slept until eight that evening. She woke up to the phone ringing. She answered it, "Hello?"

"Deidre?"

"Who is this, Renee?"

"Yes, it is me."

"How are you? I heard that you are doing well and have gotten your life back on track. I was glad to hear that."

"It's not that simple Deidre. I have just created an illusion. I think that me and you need to talk."

"We are talking Renee."

"No, I mean face to face."

"Well, I'm leaving in the morning."

"I could come by tonight."

"Renee what happened between us was wrong and it is over with, I will never betray your brother's trust again."

"I just want to talk Deidre. I just want to get some things off of my chest. It will only take a few minutes."

"Alright Renee, I'm telling you that is all that we are going to do is talk."

"That's all I want. I'm on my way over there." Renee hung up and went to Roger's room. She looked in and seen that he was sound asleep.

She snuck into his room and grabbed his car keys. She left out of the house, got into his car and headed over to Deidre's house.

Deidre did not want her mother to hear anyone knocking on the door, so she went downstairs and sat by the living room window.

She was confused when she seen Roger's car pull into the driveway, then she seen that it was Renee who was driving it. She left the window and went to the door. She opened it and stood in the doorway as Renee got out of the car and approached the house.

Deidre stepped aside to allow Renee to enter. Deidre led her over to the couch and they sat down.

"So what is it?" Deidre asked her.

"I was hoping that you could tell me."

"Tell you what?"

"Why I haven't been the same since what happened between us?" Deidre caught dejavu from hearing those words again. They were the exact words that Dianna had said to her.

"What do you mean, Roger told me that you have a boyfriend and you are happy."

"That is the furthest from the truth. I have been miserable for some time now. Having a boyfriend is just for show."

"So, you crave to be with a woman?"

"Not just any woman. I only crave for you. I have had flings with women and have felt nothing, during sex with my boyfriend, I feel nothing. For a while I thought that you had put a curse on me."

"Renee I don't know what to tell you. I haven't done anything to you, and I do not know why you are going through the things that you are going through, I am truly   sorry   about   your situation."

"Are you and my brother back together?"

"We are trying to work things out."

"What about women?"

"What about them?"

"Are you given them up?"

"Women are just as much a part of my life as men are."

"If that is the case, then you and my brother are not going to be committed to each other, and if you two are not committed to each other then it shouldn't matter who you have sex with."

"And what is your point Renee?"

"My point is I need you to fuck me." Renee told her as she stood up and began undressing. Deidre got terrified. If her mother found out what was going on downstairs she would kill Deidre.

"Renee put your clothes back on! I told you that we are not doing anything." Renee continued to take her clothes off, "I'm not leaving until you make love to me."

"Shit! … Shit! ... This bitch really is crazy" Deidre said to herself.

In a flash, Renee was standing naked in Deidre's mother's living room. Deidre ran over and started picking up Renee's clothes.

"Bring your crazy ass upstairs before you get me killed, and tip toe." she told Renee.

Renee quietly followed her upstairs and into her room. Deidre quietly closed the door and locked it. She turned to Renee, "Now what is it that you want me to do?"

"I want everything, but you can start by sucking my pussy."

"Lay your ass on the bed." Renee walked over to the bed and laid down on her back. Deidre approached her, "Take your stuff off I need to see you naked." Renee told her.

"I knew that I shouldn't have let this bitch come over here," Deidre said to herself as she started taking off her pajamas and under clothes.

She went over to the bed and dropped on her knees.

She took her hands and spread Renee's legs out, then began eating her pussy.

"Yes baby, that's what I been looking for. That's the feeling right there," Renee said as Deidre sucked her pussy.

Deidre found herself getting turned on just from eating Renee's pussy. Just the smell of her pussy aroused her. She started rising up, licking from her pussy up to her breast. She started sucking on Renee's titties and Renee started getting real vocal.

"Keep it down," Deidre told her. She rose up until they were face to face and started kissing Renee in the mouth, letting her taste her own pussy juices. Renee reached out with her hand and found Deidre's pussy. She slipped her fingers into it and started fucking her with them. Deidre sat up on Renee as if she was riding her doggy style and grinded her pussy on Renee's fingers. She reached behind her and stuck her fingers into Renee's pussy. They were both finger fucking each other. Renee started getting vocal again, "Yeah! Hell yeah! Ooh that shit feels so good." Deidre couldn't get her to quiet down, so she put a pillow over her face to drown out the noise that she was making.

They both came, then Renee forced the pillow off of her face, "Let me suck your juices," she said to Deidre. Deidre obliged her by scooting up on her face. She leaned forward with her arms extended out and her hands planted on the bed as she grinded her pussy on Renee's mouth. Renee stuck one of her fingers into Deidre's asshole as she ate her pussy. That instantly made Deidre cum all in her mouth. She came so hard that cum was running down both sides of Renee's mouth. They finished the night off with Deidre eating Renee out from the back causing her to have multiple orgasms. After they were finished they laid there on the bed for a minute, then Deidre told her, "Okay, you got what you wanted, it is time for you to go. I got to get some sleep. Your brother is taking me to the bus station in the morning."

"Okay, I'm going to leave, but you call me as soon as you get back. We are not through we are not never going to be through!"

Deidre thought about what Dianna had told her about going through some crazy shit with a girl.

"These bitches are just as crazy as the men," she said to herself. She told Renee, "Okay," just to pacify her and get her out of the house.

Chapter 25

Deidre was in a deep sleep, when she heard knocking on the door downstairs. She rolled over and looked at the clock and seen that is was 8:45 in the morning. She lifted her bedroom window and looked outside. Roger stood outside of her door.

"Geeze Roger, my bus doesn't even leave until eleven!" she yelled down to him.

"You're not taking the bus. I'm going to drive you down there. I have nothing else to do."

"You could have at least let me sleep for a few more hours."

"Haven't you had enough sleep?" Deidre did not want to let on to what had happened the night before, so she just left it alone.

"I'll be right down," she told him then closed the window.

She went downstairs and let him in. Roger tried to kiss her but she put her hand up to her mouth and pushed him away.

"I haven't even brushed my teeth yet." she told him.

"How about you go upstairs and get yourself together and I will cook you some breakfast."

"Alright, but don't mess that kitchen up. I will never hear the end of it."

"Don't worry, I got it." Deidre headed upstairs to get herself together and Roger went into the kitchen and took out some bacon and eggs. He also took out some butter and put some on a couple pieces of bread and made toast.

Deidre finished with her hygiene, got dressed, then she went downstairs and ate breakfast.

When they were done eating, they both washed the dishes and put them away. Deidre did not want to give her mother anything to complain about. When they got finished cleaning up, Roger helped her carry her things out to his car. He put them in the trunk, and then they got into the car and headed to a gas station, where Roger filled up his gas tank.

They left the gas station and hit the freeway. Roger turned on his music, and Deidre reclined her seat back and went to sleep. She slept for an hour and when she woke up Roger had the car windows down flying down the highway. A cool breeze was blowing through the open windows.

Roger looked over at Deidre, "You're up sleepy head?"

"Yes, and I feel refreshed." she told him then reached over and put her hand in his lap. Roger almost lost control of the car.

"Hey, what are you doing?"

"I always fantasized about giving you head while flying down the freeway."

"Deidre, you are crazy."

"No, I'm just horny," she told him then went for his zipper.

"She unzipped his pants and stuck her hand inside. She grabbed his dick and pulled it out of his boxers and pants. The cool breeze that was blowing into the car hit his dick and it became rock hard.

Deidre leaned over in his lap and took him into her mouth. Roger had to put both of his hands on the steering wheel to steady his self. Deidre sucked his dick as her hair blew into the wind.

Roger had to keep letting his foot up off of the gas. The head that Deidre was giving him kept causing him to press down on the gas. At one point he was doing almost seventy eight miles per hour in a sixty five an hour zone. When he started to cum, he pressed down even harder on the gas pedal, pushing the car up to eighty miles per hour. A Highway state patrol car clocked them as they sped by. He quickly got behind them and turned on his lights and siren.

"Oh shit! I'm getting pulled over!" he told Deidre. Deidre continued to milk the rest of the cum out of his dick then sat up.

When they drove past the patrolman, he had only observed one person in the car. As he drove behind Roger, all of a sudden a head popped up in the passenger's seat. It gave him an idea as to why the person driving was speeding.

Roger pulled to the side of the highway and was trying to fix his pants, when the patrolman appeared at the driver's door.

"License, registration and insurance please?"

"Sure officer," Roger said then reached across Deidre to open the glove compartment. He reached in and grabbed his registration and insurance card. He handed them to the officer, and then pulled out his wallet to retrieve his license. He handed them to the officer, who took them and went back to his ear. After about five minutes the officer came back to Roger's car and asked, "Sir, may I ask where you are heading to?"

"Yes officer, I'm on my way to take my girlfriend back to school. She goes to Ohio State University."

"Could you tell me what the emergency is then? You know that you were going fifteen miles over the speed limit."

"There is no hurry officer. It is my gas throttle, sometimes it gets stuck. I have been meaning to get it fixed."

"Your gas throttle you say?"

"Yes sir,"

"I will tell you what, I'm going to let you go with a warning this time but I advise you to get that throttle fixed as soon as possible."

"I certainly will officer."

"Okay, then you can go." he then called over to Deidre, "Oh and miss you have something on the corner of your mouth. You may want to get that." The officer told her smiling.

Roger looked over and seen that Deidre had a glob of cum hanging from the corner of her mouth.

The patrolman got back into his car and pulled off. He tipped his hat to Roger as he drove by and smiled.

Deidre licked the cum from the corner of her mouth and Roger pulled back off.

They got off the highway at a rest stop and pulled into a McDonald's. They ordered something to eat, then sat in the parking lot and ate. When they were finished eating they dumped their trash, went and used the restroom, then hopped back into the car.

When they got to Columbus, Deidre had Roger get off downtown. She directed him through downtown giving him a tour. Next she directed him to the campus and they rode around it, so that he could get familiar with it.

Roger did not know that Ohio State was as big as it was. It was more than just a college. It was also a hospital connected to it. There was a large football stadium. Roger was impressed. After the tour Deidre directed him to her dorm.

Roger parked in the student's parking lot and they grabbed her things and headed upstairs.

Deidre pulled out her keys and opened the door. They entered the room, which was empty. Deidre put her things up and they headed back out.

Deidre had Roger drive to the Ohio State fair, where they rode some rides and ate cotton candy while walking hand in hand. They also watched a concert and had a few drinks. When they left the fair and got back to the dorm Melissa was there.

She jumped off of the bed, when they entered. She ran over and hugged Deidre as if she was her long lost sister.

"Bitch let me breathe!" Deidre told her. Melissa planted kisses all over Deidre's face.

"I missed you, I'm tired of you leaving me bitch!" Deidre was going to hate to have to tell her that she would be leaving her for good soon.

Roger just stood there watching them, wondering if Melissa was her girlfriend. When they broke their embrace, Melissa looked over to Roger. She found him kind of attractive, "Where did you find him?" Melissa asked Deidre pointing to Roger.

"This is Roger, my boyfriend that I have been telling you about." Deidre said to her while winking her eye.

Melissa quickly caught on, "Oh, this is Roger? Hey Roger, Deidre talks about you so much, that I feel as if I know you personally."

"My baby did not want me catching the bus down here by myself, so he drove me." Deidre said.

"Ah, that's so sweet. We ought to take him out for that, let's go get drunk."

"You are not in a hurry to get back are you?" Deidre asked Roger.

"No, I'm not in any hurry."

"Okay bitch, get dressed. We can go out and have some drinks."

"First you have to tell me how your father is doing?"

"We will talk about it later. I do not want to spoil my mood."

"Let me get dressed, it will only take me a couple of minutes."

Melissa got dressed and they left. They had Roger take them to a club that was on campus. It had a mixed setting and a Karaoke machine. After getting drunk, Melissa got up there and started singing along to Mariah Carey. She was dancing all off beat and had everybody laughing. When she was through they gave her a round of applause.

After leaving the stage, she headed to the bathroom. Deidre told Roger, "I will be right back." She headed to the bathroom also. When she got in there Melissa was just coming out of a stall and was heading over to the sink. She walked over to her and said, "A favor for a favor."

"What the hell are you talking about?" Melissa asked Deidre.

"You say that you want me to have a threesome with you and Billy well, I want you to have one with me and Roger."

"Bitch you know that you are my girl. Shit! I will do anything for you. I'm 'bout it, 'bout it. Master P ain't got shit on me. We can do the shit right here!" Melissa said drunkenly.

"That's too much, let's go though. Let me tell you he ain't never experienced this before, so we got to put it on him."

"Don't worry I'm going to put my famous move on him."

"And what's that?"

"Eating his asshole."

"Bitch you are so stupid, let's go." They left out of the bathroom and went back out to where Roger was.

"We are ready to go baby." Roger downed the rest of his drink then said, "Let's go." They headed back to the dorm. When they got there Melissa went into the bathroom.

"You might as well stay the night and leave in the morning."

"Won't you get in trouble for that?"

"No one will know. I need me some before you go."

"What about your friend?"

"Don't worry about her." Deidre told him as she began unbuttoning his shirt. Melissa came out of the bathroom completely naked. Roger's eyes almost busted out of their sockets when he seen her walking towards him naked. He started to stutter, "Wha … Wha … What's going on?" He asked.

"Nothing is going on, it's all a dream." Deidre said to him as she went for his pants.

Melissa got behind him and helped him out of his shirt. She then bent down and started untying his shoes.

Deidre pulled his underwear and boxers down and he stepped out of them. Melissa reached her arms up under his and began rubbing his chest, "You cut up huh? Got you a few muscles." she said to him. She took one of her hands and reached through the back of his legs and fumbled with his balls.

"Nice weight but, let me see the real package." She walked to the front of him and seen that his dick was sticking up past his navel.

"See Deidre that's why I only fuck with white boys. What am I supposed to do with that, have baseball practice?" she said laughing.

"Bitch, the way your walls are torn out you can handle anything."

"You ain't got to be putting my business out there like that. Roger you wouldn't mind having some of this white chocolate would you?" Roger did not know what to say.

"It's okay boo," Deidre told him trying to get him to loosen up.

"Maybe this will loosen you up." Deidre told him then dropped down to her knees. She took him into her mouth and started sucking him off. He did not know how Melissa did it, but somehow she got up under Deidre and started sucking his balls.

She had them in her mouth rolling them around inside of it. Roger looked down at both of them, and could not believe what was going on. Fred had told him that it felt like dying and going to heaven. He did not know about the dying part, but Roger did feel like he was in heaven. He opened his legs and squatted a little bit so that Melissa could have more room to suck his balls.

Deidre and Melissa switched positions and Melissa starred giving him head. Melissa gave him sloppy head. She used a lot of saliva. She spit on his dick and slurped on it. Her technique was different from Deidre's, but it felt just as good, if not better.

Deidre stood up, walked over to the bed and got doggy style on it. She looked back over her shoulder, "Come on boo, and give it to me." Melissa let go of Roger's dick and he walked over to the bed. He got onto the bed on his knees behind Deidre. He guided his dick into her and started fucking her. He long dicked her, fucking her slowly and she was loving it. She was making all types of fuck faces, and biting down on her forefinger.

All of a sudden Roger felt something wet in the crack of his asshole. He jumped, "What the hell!" He looked back and Melissa was there smiling, "What the fuck are you doing?" he asked her.

"I'm giving you my famous rim job." She said giggling.

"No way, I don't play that. Stay away from my ass!"

"You're no fun. Why do you guys get so scared about your little poop chute. I think that you all be scared that you might like it."

"I don't care anything about what you're saying. Just keep your mouth and your hands away from my ass. You don't want me fucking around with your ass!"

"You do not know me very well. I welcome you to stick your big dick in my asshole, plus you won't need any lube." Roger thought to himself, "This white bitch is crazy." Roger looked at Deidre. "That's one crazy white girl."

"We got to let her in boo or she is going to get on our nerves. I'll tell you what lie down, I want to sit on your face." Roger laid down flat on the bed and Deidre mounted his face.

Melissa mounted his dick facing Deidre. They both rode him while they explored each other's breast with their bands and kissed each other in the mouth. Melissa wanted to show Roger that she was serious about what she said. She lifted herself up off of his dick, took her hand and guided his dick to the entrance of her asshole. She slowly sunk down onto him. Fred immediately knew that something was different. The feeling that he was getting from her pussy had change. He was getting a super-hot and tight feeling around his dick. He could not see what was going on because Deidre was riding his face.

"Let him see Deidre. I want him to see this." Deidre climbed off of Roger and he lifted his head, "Watch," She told him as she spun around on his dick without him coming out of her. She came up until she had her feet flat on the bed. She put her hands on his thighs, leaned forward. She was in a squatting position and started riding his dick.

Roger watched fascinated as he watched how her asshole muscles clung to his dick. She was riding him as if his dick was inside of her pussy.

"This how white girls do it." she said as she slammed down on his dick. Roger couldn't hold it anymore. He thought that he shot about a pint of cum up into her asshole.

Melissa was proud of her handy work. She got up and headed into the bathroom to clean herself up.

Roger looked at Deidre, "That's one crazy white girl."

"Yeah that's my dawg,"

When Melissa came out of the bathroom, they went in there and took a shower together. Afterwards they climbed into the bed and went to sleep.

Ÿ

The next morning Roger took Deidre out for breakfast. After that he took her back to her dorm then hit the highway.

As he drove he said to himself, "Having a bisexual girl ain't bad at all.

Chapter 26

Deidre went back to school, and studied with a vengeance. She was determined to get ahead on her school work, so that she could get home sooner. She did not even go back to work, because she wanted to put all of her concentration into school.

She and Melissa were in their room one night studying, when Melissa said, "How about this weekend?"

"How about what this weekend?"

"You know the threesome."

"Melissa, I need to study this weekend."

"You said that last weekend and the weekend before, Billy keeps nagging me and I am getting sick of it. I just want to get the whole thing over with. When you asked me I did not hesitate, but you keep brushing me off." Deidre sat there staring into her book. Truthfully she wasn't feeling too good. For the last couple of weeks she had been feeling sick. She even had to rush to the bathroom to vomit a few times.

She was sick of hearing Melissa's crying, so she decided to go ahead and get it out of the way.

"Alright damn! Set it up for this weekend." she told Melissa with more attitude than she intended to show.

"You ain't got to get all funky about it."

"I'm sorry Melissa, I just have a lot on my mind and I haven't been feeling too well lately. Go ahead and set it up for this weekend and we will take care of poor Billy." Melissa went over to Deidre and gave her a hug and kissed her on the cheek.

"You know I love you girl. You are like my sister from another mother. We look just alike don't we?" Melissa said laughing. Deidre had to start laughing too. Melissa was one of the silliest and coolest white girls that she had ever met.

Saturday came and Billy came to pick them up in his 1983 Chevy Camaro. There was no paint on the car at all. The whole car was covered in primer. When Deidre seen Billy she thought to herself, "All you have to do is put hill in front of his name." To her Billy looked just like a hillbilly. He had long oily hair and a tooth missing in the front. When he spoke, "Hey there chocolate," that took the cake. Deidre could not figure out how in the hell Melissa had hooked up with him.

They got into his car, with Deidre climbing into the backseat. When Billy started the car it rumbled. The engine was very loud. It was as if the car did not have a muffler system at all. The powerful engine caused the car to shake. Deidre felt like her brain was rattling inside of her head.

By the time they got to the bar, she thought that she was getting off of a roller coaster ride. It took a while for the vibrating sensation to leave her body.

They entered into a hick bar, where Deidre found that she was the only black person there. Some people gave the group strange looks, but nobody said anything to them.

They found a table and a waitress came to take their orders. Billy ordered them a round of Bud Light beer and some peanuts.

Deidre thought to herself, "This ain't going to get it. I'm going to have to be drunk, real drunk to do something with him." She called out to another waitress. She told the waitress to bring her two doubles of Jack Daniels straight.

"You like that strong stuff huh girly?" Billy asked her. Deidre just shook her head.

"Lissa here told me that you agreed to have a threesome with us, I was kind of leery at first. I have never had sex with a black gal before, but she says that you are clean, so I guess I will take my chances."

"Oh no he didn't!" Deidre said to herself. She looked over to Melissa, "Let me talk to you for a minute." They both slid their chairs back and got up from the table. They walked towards the restroom, and when they got in there Deidre asked her, "Bitch what is wrong with that cracker. You are trying to get me to have sex with a member of the Klu Klux Klan."

"Billy is not in no Klan. You just have to get use to him that's all."

"Listen, if hillbilly Billy says one more stupid thing out of his mouth the shit is off!" With that being said, Deidre walked out of the bathroom.

They got back to the table and Billy asked them, "Is everything okay?"

"Yeah, everything is okay." Melissa told him.

"Well do you want to order some more drinks. I'm ready to get this thing started. I can't wait to have me some of that dark meat. I heard that those dark women fuck like animals. Some aren't even tamed. I'm sure she will love this white cock and that she will go and tell all of her dark friends about it."

"Hold up mother fucker! That's it. You aren't going to keep sitting up here in my face disrespecting me. And for the record I wouldn't tell my friends if I did fuck your little dick white ass! Yeah that's right little dick, Melissa told me. You pee wee Herman looking mother fucker."

"Lissa what the hell is wrong with this coon friend of yours?"

"Billy, what is wrong with you? How could you treat my friend like this?"

"This black gal ain't your friend and if my momma and her sister knew about this they would disown you." Deidre wondered what that comment meant. She was sure going to question Melissa about it later on, but right then she had to get up out of there before she caught a case or they tried to lynch her.

"Melissa I'm gone, I will see you back at the room."

"Go on ahead monkey, swing on some branches all the way back across town." Billy yelled after her.

"You are just plain stupid Billy, you are a retard!"

"You better gone ahead and get out of here with your nigger friend. If you weren't my cousin, I would kick your nigger loving ass." Melissa left out of the bar and caught up with Deidre.

Deidre was walking with a purpose, trying to get out of that neighborhood as fast as she could. It was hard for Melissa to keep up with her, because of the heels that she was wearing.

"I'm so sorry Deidre. I swear I did not know that he would act like that."

"Who is he and where did you meet him at?"

"He is my cousin."

"He's your damn cousin! And you have been fucking him?"

"I'm originally from West Virginia and that is how things are down there. Me and Billy have been fucking since we were kids."

"That is so gross!"

"Deidre don't judge me. I haven't judged you for any of the things that you have done"

"I'm not judging you. I just said it's gross."

They walked until they were out of that neighborhood and on a main street. When they saw a taxi, they flagged it down and got a ride back to the dorm.

Chapter 27

Deidre was ahead of schedule with her school work. She had two more exams to take and she would be able to get home almost a month earlier.

She was walking through campus one day, when she heard someone call her name. "Deidre, hey Deidre." She turned and seen that it was Helen calling her. She turned and walked towards her. She had not seen Helen since she had passed out of her class. She had been meaning to get in touch with her but so much had been going on.

"Deidre, how are you dear?"

"I'm okay Helen, how are you?"

"I'm fine, me and Henry have been wondering about you for some time now. You promised to keep in touch, but we haven't heard from you."

"I know that I did not keep my word and I'm so sorry. I have been going through so much."

"Where are you on your way to right now? I was just going to the library."

"How about we go for a cup of coffee or a drink and talk?"

"We can do that." They walked to the staff's parking lot and got into Helen's BMW. She drove them to a little coffee shop, where they ordered coffee and donuts.

"So tell me what has been going on with you Deidre."

"Well I have been trying to get ahead on my work, so that I can get my credits transferred. I'm moving back home. My father was in a terrible accident and had to have one of his legs removed, and I have to move back home to help my mother take care of him."

"Deidre, I am so sorry to hear that. I know that Henry will feel the same way when he finds out. You know that he is quite fond of you?"

"I am fond of you both and am grateful for the things that you two did for me."

"Maybe we can do more. Maybe there is something we can do to help your situation."

"I do not think that there is anything that you can do, plus you two have done enough for me already."

"When are you leaving?"

"I will be leaving within the next two weeks."

"Deidre you must come and see us before you go, you just must."

"How about next weekend, I could spend my last weekend up here with you."

"That would be marvelous dear. I can't wait to tell Henry. We will come and pick you up from your dorm Friday around eight, is that alright?"

"Yes, that will be fine Helen," They finished their coffee and donuts and Helen took her back to the campus and dropped her off in front of the library so that she could go and study for her test.

Ÿ

The following Friday, Helen and Henry picked Deidre up. They took her out to dinner, where they sat and talked.

Deidre filled Henry in on the things that she had told Helen.

"Deidre if there is anything that me and Henry can do to help you let us know. Anything you can think of, you do not be scared to ask us you here?"

"Yes, I hear you Henry and I appreciate your concern. They finished their dinner and ordered some wine. After that they headed home. Helen led Deidre to the same room that she had before. Deidre put her things away then went back downstairs.

They all sat and talked for a while. Around eleven o'clock Henry and Helen decided to call it a night. They both were concerned about what Deidre was going through, so they did not want to pressure her into doing anything. Just having her there was good enough for them.

They did however decide to enjoy each other. They got naked and got into bed. Henry laid back with his arms folded behind his head as Helen sucked him off.

Deidre did not like sitting alone downstairs in that big house. She decided to head up to her room. Once she got upstairs she got curious as to what Henry and Helen were doing. She walked to the room and seen that that door was closed. She put her ear to the door and tried to eavesdrop.

She thought that she heard muffled sounds. She turned the door knob and eased the door open. All she seen was Helen's pussy and ass rose up in the air. She could tell that Helen was giving Henry head from the way that the front part of her body kept lowering and rising.

"Deidre my darling, do come in and join us." Henry said to her. Deidre walked over to the bed. She stood at the end of the bed and took off all of her clothes. She climbed on to the bed behind Helen and started eating her from the back. Helen started wiggling her ass and pushing it back onto Deidre's mouth as she sucked Henry off.

Deidre took both of her hands and spread Helen's ass cheeks apart so that she could devour her pussy.

"Helen please let me up so that I can tend to Deidre's pussy." Helen let Henry up and she rolled over onto her back. Deidre went back to eating her pussy and Henry stood off of the bed behind Deidre and entered her from the back.

"Ah yes! I have missed this pussy so … So much." he said as he sunk into her.

He fucked her slowly, "Oh how I love fucking your young pussy Deidre. So sweet, so tender." Deidre moaned into Helen's pussy. She loved the way that Henry would take his time fucking her. The combination of the way that he fucked her and the way that he talked to her while fucking her kept her cumming.

"Sorry my dear, but I must invade your bugger. I have to fuck this young asshole of yours." Henry said to Deidre as he popped his dick out of her pussy and positioned it at her asshole. He put the head at the entrance and pushed in. At first he met resistance, then after applying a little more pressure the head popped in.

A searing pain shot through Deidre's body and she fell forward lying flat on her stomach with her face in Helen's chest.

Henry fell right along with her not letting his dick come out of her. He just laid there on top of Deidre for a few minutes letting her asshole adjust to his dick. When he felt that she had adjusted enough, he started fucking her ass in a slow rhythm. Deidre whimpered into Helen's chest as he fucked her asshole. Helen rubbed her hair as her head laid on her chest.

"You will be okay deary. When Henry first started butt fucking me, I couldn't take it, now I love it."

Henry pulled Deidre's hips up so that he could get better penetration. He started fucking her asshole as if it was a pussy, and Deidre started responding to it. The pain soon turned to pleasure and she wanted more of it. She started pushing her ass up meeting his thrust.

When, she would go down she would tighten her ass muscles sucking him in. Henry started to lose control. He knew that he wouldn't be able to last much longer, so he picked up his pace and started fucking her asshole with forced. He tightened up and shot his load into her. Deidre was surprised to find herself cumming when he started cumming in her asshole.

Ÿ

For the rest of the weekend they did many things from going out shopping to going to see a play. Sunday evening when they were about to take Deidre back to her dorm, they gave her a check for ten thousand dollars.

"I cannot take this!" Deidre told them after she seen what it was.

"That's nonsense that is a gift from us to you. Use it as you see fit. It may come in handy covering some of your father's expenses."

"Deidre gave both of them hugs and thanked them. They dropped her off at the dorm and she went in and started packing.

Later that night Melissa came in and seen all of her bags packed. The realization set in that Deidre was leaving. They had been roommates for almost two years, and Melissa had become very fond of her.

She flopped down onto her bed. "So how are you getting home?"

"Roger is coming to pick me up tomorrow."

"I'm sure going to miss you Dee." Melissa told her as tears formed at the corners of her eyes.

"I'm going to miss you too girl, but don't start that sensitive shit!" she told her as she found herself getting choked up.

"Let's not make this a sad moment then, let's celebrate." Melissa said then got up off of her bed. She went to her small refrigerator and pulled out a bottle of Vodka. She grabbed two dixy cups and went and sat on Deidre's bed. She opened the Vodka and poured them drinks.

They sat on the bed drinking and reminiscing about all of the fun that they had together since they had been roommates.

They were talking when all of a sudden Deidre felt the urge to throw up. She jumped up off of the bed and ran towards the bathroom.

"What's wrong Dee?" Melissa yelled as she jumped up and followed behind her. When she got to the bathroom door, Deidre was bent over the toilet vomiting.

"Girl you ain't even drinking that much to be throwing up like that." After Deidre emptied her stomach, she went to the sink and brushed her teeth. She rinsed her mouth out then told Melissa, "It's something else. It's not the liquor. This is my fourth time throwing up this week."

"Girl, you might be pregnant."

"Bitch, don't be cursing me like that."

"You said yourself that you have been feeling sick a lot lately and have been throwing up. To me they are signs of being pregnant." The more that Deidre thought about it the more that she thought that it might be true.

"I'm going to the drugstore the first thing in the morning to pick up a pregnancy test."

"Grab two of them just to make sure. Sometimes those things give false readings."

Deidre hardly slept that night. She was too anxious to find out if she was pregnant or not.

At nine o'clock she got up, took a shower and put on her clothes. She left her room and headed to a drugstore. When she got to the store she requested that the sales clerk give her two pregnancy tests. The clerk rang the test up and she paid for them and left. She walked fast back to her room.

When she got there Melissa was sitting up in her bed. She watched as Deidre rushed into the bathroom. She got out of her bed and went to the bathroom. When she opened the door, Deidre was squatting over the toilet pissing onto the stick.

"Damn bitch! Can I have some privacy?"

"You ain't been needing any privacy. It ain't like I ain't seen all of your private parts. I want to see what that stick reads." Deidre stood up and pulled her panties and pants back up. She looked at the color on the stick, "Dammit!"

"What does it say?"

"That I'm pregnant. I don't believe this shit."

"Do it again just to make sure." Deidre grabbed the other test, pulled her clothes back down and pissed on the stick. She pulled her clothes back up and sat the stick on top of the sink. She sat back down on the toilet for five minutes. She got up and picked the stick up. It had the same reading as the first.

"Well it's official."

"Do you know who you're pregnant by?"

"Bitch! Of course I know who I'm pregnant by." she thought back to her trip home. She knew that she could not be pregnant by anyone except Roger. The big question that she had to ask herself was if she was ready to have a kid. With trying to help her father, wanting to finish school and have a career and not being ready to settle down with one sex, she did not know if it was the right time to have a baby.

She thought about not telling anyone and just getting an abortion. She thought about using some of the money that she had gotten from Henry and Helen. She knew that her mother wouldn't approve of her having an abortion because of her religion. She did not know how Roger would feel. She was not even sure how she felt.

Could she settle down and be a mother. Could she raise a kid living the type of lifestyle that she was living. She thought about it and came to the conclusion that she had done almost everything that could be done sexually. What else was it that she could do. One thing popped up in her head. She had yet to have sex with two girls at one time, "That could be my going out with a bang party. Maybe after that I can settle down." she said to herself.

Melissa interrupted her thoughts, "If you keep it I want to be the Godmother, I asked you first."

"Do you think that we are ever going to see each other again after I leave?"

"I don't see why not. Bitch I will come visit your ass if you stayed on the moon." Deidre started laughing, "Okay girl, if I have it you have my word that I will make you the Godmother."

"That's all a bitch ask for." Melissa told her.

Chapter 28

There was a knock at the door and Deidre went and opened it. There stood Roger with a big smile on his face. He was smiling as if he knew what they had just gotten through talking about. Deidre walked over to him and gave him a hug. He put his arms around her waist and gave her a big kiss. He released her and said, "Are you ready to go?"

"Yeah, we just got to put all my things in the car."

"Don't worry about that. Say your goodbyes to your friend and I will load your things up in the car." Roger started picking up her bags and carrying them down to his car. He had to make four trips. Lucky for him Deidre had decided to leave her portable refrigerator and hot plate.

Deidre and Melissa exchanged numbers and gave each other a farewell hug and kiss, then Deidre and Roger got into his car and he pulled off heading back to Cleveland.

They were riding down the freeway when Deidre turned to him and said, "I'm pregnant." Roger put a horrified look on his face.

"How could you do this to me Deidre? You could of used protection. How could you get pregnant on me?"

"Deidre wanted to hit Roger in his face for being so stupid.

"I'm pregnant by you dummy!" Roger started cheesing, "For real?"

"Yeah for real! It had to happen when I came home for that visit, I haven't been to the doctor yet, but after I get settled in we can go to the doctor, so that I can find out how far along I am and you can do the math."

"I can't believe it. I'm going to be a father. There is so much that we have to do. We got to find a place, pick a name and set a date."

"Whoa, set a date for what Roger?"

"For us to get married."

"Roger, you are moving way to fast. All that about finding a house and us getting married. I'm not ready for those things yet. I'm not ready to settle down. I knew that you would say the things that you are saying that's why I had thoughts of having an abortion."

"Abortion! You would have killed my baby without telling me. You would do something that cold?"

"I thought about it, because I did not want to go through what you are putting me through now. I'm telling you that I'm not ready to move in with you and I really do not plan on getting married anytime soon."

"So how are we supposed to do this Deidre?"

"Do what?"

"Raise our child?"

"We do not have to live together or get married to raise a child together."

"To give a child a fair opportunity to make it in this world it needs to have a two parent home."

"Well, I'm not ready for that right now. We have plenty of time to discuss all of that. Right now I just want a piece of mind."

Roger drove the rest of the way in silence. He was frustrated and trying to figure out how to get through to Deidre. He figured that maybe he needed to talk to her parents. He thought that maybe they could persuade her to do what was right.

Deidre sat back with her eyes closed. She was trying to figure out things in her head. How could she make things work? The only person that she felt that she could confide in without being judged was her father. She decided that she would have a talk with him.

When they got to Cleveland, Roger drove straight to Deidre's parent's house. He pulled into their driveway and cut the car off. They got out of the car and went to his trunk. He popped it and they started pulling her things out.

Deidre noticed that her mother's car was not in the driveway and felt relief. She pulled out her house key and opened the door.

They started taking her things into the house.

"Deidre is that you?" her father called to her. He came rolling out of the kitchen in a wheelchair.

Deidre sat her bags down and ran over to him, "Daddy you're home!" she said to him as she gave him a hug.

"I have been home for two weeks now. I have been trying to get use to all these contraptions.

"You mean the wheelchair?"

"Hell, this is the least of it. I have a pair of crutches, a walker and even a fake leg. I cannot get use to the leg right now because where they cut my leg off at has not healed enough yet and trying to use the leg causes the area to start bleeding, which can cause infection. I will be glad when I can get out of this wheelchair though. It makes me feel trapped."

"You're going to be okay daddy. I'm here to help take care of you."

"That's just it Deidre, I do not want to be taken care of. I have always been independent and whenever I can use that damn leg I will do things on my own again."

Deidre understood how her father was feeling. He had never had to depend on anyone for anything. He had been taking care of his self since he was fifteen years old.

Roger brought the last of her bags into the house. He stood around waiting to see if Deidre was going to say anything to him. After seeing that she was completely ignoring him and just carrying her bags upstairs. He turned and left out of the house closing the door behind him.

Deidre put all of her things away, then went back downstairs and found her father sitting in the living room watching television. She went and sat on the couch.

"Daddy we need to talk, I need your guidance." Her father turned his chair so that he was facing her, "Sure sugar, what you need to talk about?"

"I'm pregnant," Deidre's father beamed with pride. He had a big smile on his face.

"I'm going to be a granddaddy?"

"Yes you are,"

"What is the problem Deidre?"

"I'm not ready to settle down."

"You don't want to have the baby?"

"It's not that, I'm not ready to live with no man or get married."

"And who says that you have to do all of that?"

"Nobody says that I have to do it, but it's what Roger wants to do and you know how mom is going to feel about me having a baby out of wedlock."

"Deidre there is not going to be anything that comes between you having my grandbaby. Not Roger and not your mother. We will help you take care of the baby until you decide that you are ready to settle down, that's if you ever decide that you are ready to settle down."

That is why Deidre loved her father, she knew that he would support her no matter what, "Do you think I should tell mom?"

"Of course you should tell her. We will both tell her tonight at dinner." Deidre felt that as long as her father had her back that it would not be too bad.

"I'm going to go and take me a shower then I'm going to make dinner."

"That sounds good, your mother has been TV dinnering me to death, I could go for a nice cooked meal."

Deidre went upstairs and showered. Afterwards she went down to the kitchen and into the refrigerator to see what her mother had in there to cook.

She decided to cook some chicken breast, rice and some macaroni and cheese. She was still cooking when her mother came into the house. Her mother instantly smelled the food.

"Earl who is cooking? That food smells delicious."

"That's Deidre honey, she came home today. She has some wonderful news too."

"Oh, does she? Well let me go upstairs and get out of these clothes and shoes. I'll be back down in a minute." Carolynn went upstairs to change out of her work clothes and her high heeled shoes.

"Deidre," her father called out. Deidre came out of the kitchen, "Yes daddy?"

"You might as well set the table, your mother is here. We better go ahead and give her the news."

"Okay, I will set the table, dinner is ready." Deidre headed back into the kitchen and started fixing the plates and setting the table.

Her mother wheeled her father into the kitchen and they took their plates. Deidre sat plates of extra food on the table, and then took her seat at the table.

Her mother went straight in, "So Deidre your father says that you have some good news, what is it?"

"I'm pregnant,"

"You're pregnant! Praise God, he must of answered my prayers. I have prayed every night that you leave that lifestyle that you have been living alone. The Lord has answered my prayers. So who is the father?"

"Roger is the father."

"And when do you two plan on getting married?"

"That's just it I don't plan on marrying Roger anytime soon."

"You cannot bring a bastard child into this world Deidre. You need to marry that man and raise your child properly."

"Ma, I haven't left that lifestyle as you referred to it alone. I still am attracted to women and I'm not ready to settle down with no man."

"You shut up! Just shut up! Earl you need to talk some sense into this child. She has lost her mind. She likes women, is pregnant by a man, but does not want to be with a man. What type of nonsense is that?"

"It's her life Carolynn. She is a grown woman. I'm going to support her 100%."

"Well, I am not! I do not condone the way that she is living, and I do not want her living under this roof if she plans to keep living in sin."

"Fine mother, I will find me a place to live tomorrow. I am grown and I can take care of myself."

"I cannot tell that you are grown. You are still acting like a child."

"I tried daddy, I really tried. I love you but I cannot stay in this house with her. I'm going to find me a place tomorrow. A place that's close enough so that I can still come and check on you."

"Do you need any money?"

"No, I will be fine."

"You know they gave me the insurance money for the car. You can take it to get you a car."

"I have enough to take care of everything right now. If later I find that I need some more money, I will let you know. I'm going to bed." she told him then headed upstairs.

"Be out of this house by tomorrow!" her mother yelled after her. Deidre continued up to her room. She slammed her door and fell on her bed crying.

Downstairs her father told her mother, "Carolynn, you're the devil in the flesh. All that crap about the Bible. You are just evil."

"Whatever Earl! I'm going to bed." Deidre's mother told him as she headed to her room.

Deidre's father wished that he had his leg so that he could go up the steps to comfort Deidre. Since his leg had been removed, the downstairs den was turned into his room.

He and his wife were no longer sharing the same bed. Tears formed at the corners of his eyes as he wheeled himself to his room. To see his daughter hurt caused him to hurt.

Chapter 29

The next day Deidre called Dianna to come take her to look at some houses that she had picked out of a newspaper and to take her to buy herself a car.

She did not feel like being bothered with Roger, that was why she called Dianna. Dianna went and picked her up and they went and viewed the houses. Deidre settled for a small two bedroom house that was only three blocks away from her father's house. She paid the security deposit and the first month's rent and got the keys from the landlord.

Next she had Dianna take her car shopping. They drove up and down the auto mile looking at and test driving cars. Deidre settled on a Dodge Neon.

She put forty five hundred down and agreed to pay notes on it. After the paperwork was completed and her car was fitted with a temporary license plate, Deidre headed to a furniture store with Dianna following her. Deidre bought a bedroom set and a living room set and found that she only had six hundred dollar left from the money that Henry and Helen had given her. She figured that was enough to get her gas, phone and electricity turned on at the house.

She knew that she was going to have to find a job quickly. The furniture store agreed to deliver her furniture to the house first thing in the morning.

She and Dianna decided to go and have some lunch. They drove out to Red Lobster and ordered a seafood platter. They sat there, ate and talked. Deidre told her that she was pregnant and how her mother and Roger were acting.

"I guess I'm lucky. My mom and pop both support me. Hopefully your mom will come around soon. You have to do what you feel is right for you though. You are the only one that has to live your life. You can't let your mother nor Roger dictate how you live your life." Deidre told her.

I still have to find a place to stay until they turn my utilities on tomorrow."

"Girl you can stay with me. I got a nice apartment. There is only one bedroom though. You will have to sleep with me unless you want to sleep on the couch." Dianna told her then looked towards her to see what her reaction would be.

Deidre knew that Dianna was trying to find out if she wanted to have sex with her. She did not bite. She figured if something happened, that it just happened.

Dianna followed Deidre to her parent's home so that she could get a few of her things. When Deidre entered the house her father was hopping around on some crutches.

"Daddy! What are you doing?"

"Learning to be more mobile. I can't just sit in that damn thing all day."

"What if you fall?"

"If I fall I will get back up dammit! Do not treat me like a kid Deidre, I will be okay. Now did you find a place?"

"Yes, I found a place a couple of blocks from here. I bought a car and I got me some furniture."

"Where did you get all of that money from?"

"A couple of my friends looked out for me when they found out I was coming back home."

"Shit! I wish that I had friends like that."

"Well, I'm broke now."

"How much do you need?"

"Just some spending money, so that I can get around until I find a job."

"I'll tell you what, I will just give you my credit card, that way you can use it as needed."

"Thank you daddy."

"Don't worry about it sweetie. I'll tell you this make sure you got a room for me at your house, because if your mother keeps up with her bullshit, I will be moving in with you."

"You know that you will always be welcome daddy." she told him then went over to him and gave him a kiss.

Her and Dianna left, and she followed Dianna to her house. When they got there, she saw that Dianna had a nice one bedroom apartment. It was real cozy. They were not in the house for two minutes before the phone started ringing.

Dianna answered it then screwed her face up. She began a conversation, "My cellphone must be off. I will have to check it."

"Where are you at?"

"I'm at home,"

"Let's go out and find a girl?"

"I do not feel like going out tonight."

"You have been playing me off a lot lately. What you don't want to fuck with me no more?"

"I don't want to argue with you Fred."

"My friend is over here and I just want to spend some time with her."

"Oh I see you're trying to get down without me."

"Fred you know what it's over between us. You want a three way take your ass down to the bar by yourself. Matter of fact take your ass to a men's gay bar and pick you up two men. I'm sick of your shit. Don't call here no more!"

"Fuck you bitch!"

"No fuck your little dick ass!" Dianna told him then slammed the phone down.

"Girl, what was all that about?" Deidre asked her.

"That was Fred I'm tired of his ass. Every night he wants to go out and find a girl to have a three way with. He turned into a straight monster. It was just really me luring the girls in for his enjoyment. That shit is dead and over with. Come on let me show you my room." They both headed to Dianna's room.

Deidre entered the room and thought that she had entered into a sex chamber. There was a canopy bed in the middle of the floor. Mirrors covered the walls, chains with handcuffs at the end of them hung from her wall. There were all type of toys around the room and she had a rack that was filled with costumes.

"What do you do with all of this stuff?" Deidre asked her as she looked around the room in amazement.

"This is my fantasy room. All fantasies and desires can be fulfilled in this room." Deidre walked over to her dresser and picked up a pink two headed dildo that curved up on both ends, "Interesting," she said to herself. She put it down, and then picked up a gigantic black dildo that had a large pair of life like balls attached to it.

"Girl you sure have become sexually free."

"Yeah, I have become sexually liberated."

"What do you do, put on sex shows or something?"

"Me and Fred would have girls over and we would do some role playing." Deidre walked over to the rack and started looking through the costumes. She saw that there were cheerleading outfits, nurse's outfits, catholic school outfits. There was even a playboy bunny outfit.

Deidre realized that Dianna had come a long way from the girl who had gone ballistic when she sucked her pussy.

"Do you like it?" Dianna asked her.

"It's cool, I might have to get me a few things for my place."

"I can get you hooked up. Girl, I got whips, balls and chains. I even got a chastity belt."

"Dianna you are too much."

"You use to intimidate me. I'll tear your ass up now though." Dianna told her.

"You still can't fuck with me!"

"Shit, I got moves that will make you cum in two minutes."

"I have to see those moves then." Deidre told her.

"Let me put something on TV before I go and get a few things." Dianna grabbed a remote and hit a button. A projection screen descended from the ceiling. She hit another button and on came the projector. On the screen showed people having an orgy. People were in a room fucking everywhere. In some places there were three and four people engaged in sex together.

"Make yourself comfortable," Dianna told her then left the room.

When Dianna re-entered the room she had a lit burning candle in her hand. She sat the candle down on a table next to the bed. She went over to her dresser and grabbed a long, slim piece of rubber that looked too small to be a vibrator. She grabbed a couple bottles of oil off of her dresser then headed over to the bed.

"I know you have been stressing, so how about I give you a full body massage to get some of that tension out of your body. Take your clothes off and lay on the bed while I change into something more comfortable." Dianna went over to the rack, grabbed a costume and left out of the room.

Deidre stripped out of her clothes and laid down on the bed watching the porno. Dianna came back into the room wearing a crotchless bunny costume.

Deidre looked up and seen Dianna's perfectly shaved pussy and her mouth began to water. Dianna went over to the bed and sat down next to Deidre. She picked up a bottle and squirted some of the substance out of it into her hands. She rubbed her hands together, and then put them on Deidre's arms.

She started massaging the substance into Deidre's arms and a warming, tingling sensation started going through Deidre's arms. She took the bottle and put it over Deidre's back and squirted some onto her back. Then she squirted some down both of her legs. She started massaging the substance into her skin. Everywhere that she rubbed the substance on, it became warm and tingling to Deidre.

She did Deidre's whole back then had her turn over to do the front. The substance had her titties and her pussy on fire. Deidre did not know what was going on, she just knew that she was feeling good all over.

Dianna got up off of the bed and went and grabbed a strap on dildo. She strapped on the dildo then went and climbed onto the bed.

"Get on your hands and knees," she told Deidre. Deidre got up and assumed the doggy style position. Dianna squirted some of the substance in her hand and rubbed it up and down the length of the dildo.

She positioned herself behind Deidre and inserted the head of the dildo inside of her. When the heat hit the insides of Deidre's pussy her body shook.

"Fuck! What is that shit?"

"Don't worry just enjoy the ride." Dianna told her as she started fucking her. Deidre's body was on fire. It was as if she could not be still. She needed to be doing something. She took one of her hands and reached between her legs and began playing with her clit while Dianna fucked her.

Dianna reached over to the table and picked up the candle. She brought it over Deidre's back and tipped it. Drops of candle wax landed on Deidre's back.

"Oh my God! Fuck!" Deidre said out loud. Dianna made a trail down her back with the candle wax. To Deidre it was pain and pleasure. She started bucking back onto the dildo.

Dianna set the candle down and picked up the long rubber piece. She rubbed some of the substance up and down it, and then put it to Deidre's asshole entrance. At the end of the rubber was a control knob and Dianna turned it on. The piece of rubber came to life. It vibrated as Dianna stuck it into Deidre's ass.

"Gosh no! I can't take it. Di, please stop!"

"You're a big girl you can handle it." Dianna told her as she pushed the anal vibrator further into her ass. When she sunk the vibrator all the way in, she turned the speed up, and left the vibrator deep in her ass as she began fucking her with a deep thrust.

"Fuck! … Fuck! … Fuck!" Deidre yelled as she felt her climax coming. There was so much tension building up in her body that when she erupted she instantly got a headache.

Her head started pounding and she started feeling lightheaded. She put her head down on the bed and closed her eyes trying to will the headache away. Dianna squirted more of the substance onto both the vibrator and the dildo, as she fucked her with them she found herself cumming again.

After the second mind boggling orgasm she couldn't take anymore. She crawled off of the dildo that Dianna had strapped on and got up off the bed and left out of the room with the anal vibrator still stuck in her ass. Indeed Dianna had proven that she had skills.

Chapter 30

Deidre moved into her house. It felt good to have a place of her own. She went and got her a job at OfficeMax and enrolled back in school. She had gotten herself a prenatal doctor. She was four months pregnant and was starting to show.

She thought that she had made a mistake by letting Roger know where she stayed. He somehow kept finding ways to come over there and get on her nerves. All he did was try to pamper her and tell her what she should and should not do concerning the baby.

He always found a way to make her feel guilty and have sex with him.

Two things she wouldn't bulge on at first was letting him move in with her and accepting his proposals.

One day he came over and brought Renee with him. Renee came into the house and acted like everything was okay.

She said that she couldn't wait to her niece or nephew came into the world. She asked when they were going to find out if it was going to be a boy or a girl, so that she can start buying clothes and toys.

Roger thought that what had happened with her and Deidre was a thing of the past.

Renee played the part as best as she could, but she could not wait to be alone with Deidre.

Deidre would go around to her parent's house whenever she had free time and her mother was not there, so that she could check on her father. He was getting around pretty good with his prosthetic leg. When Deidre would come over, he would tell her, "Let's go."

"Where are we going?"

"Anywhere but here!" He would have her take him to run errands and out to the park to watch softball games. Deidre did not mind. She did not much care for softball, but she loved spending time with her father.

They were watching a game one day and she told him, "I'm having a boy. You know that I'm naming him Earl."

Deidre's father put a smile on his face as wide as the front end of a Cadillac.

"I'm going to have a grandson to play catch with. I can teach him how to ride a bike, we can go fishing. I'm going to get him a bracelet with his name on it."

"Daddy, slow down. You are getting outrageous. He's not even here yet."

"It's never too early to start planning."

"I been thinking too."

"Thinking about what?"

"I been thinking about maybe settling down with Roger. What do you think?"

"I think you need to do whatever makes you happy. Do not do something just for the formality of it, or for the wrong reasons. Anything that's not based off of the right reasons won't last. Now you take what I have said and make your own decision."

"That's fair." she told him. She figured that maybe it was time to slow down and settle down. After what Dianna had done to her she could not see herself giving up women. Maybe she and Roger could work something out where they could share women like they had done with Melissa. She thought back to what Dianna told her about Fred. She did not think that Roger would turn into a monster like Fred did, but she knew that you never could tell.

She met with Roger and they discussed the situation. Roger was willing to agree with anything just to have a stable relationship with Deidre.

She told him, "Look I'm not ready for marriage, but I am willing to try living together as a couple. Only thing is, you are going to have to accept me for who I am. Can you accept me having sex with women?"

"If it does not get out of hand and is not done behind my back then yeah, I can deal with it."

"Okay then, give me a couple weeks, then you can move in." They both agreed that he would move in and that they would see how things worked out.

Deidre decided to go out with a bang. One day when Renee was over there visiting with Roger. She told her to find a way over to her house Friday night. She also called and invited Dianna over Friday night. She even told Dianna to bring some of her toys, which she agreed to do.

Friday night came and Renee showed up first. They were sitting on the couch and Renee asked her, "So what did you invite me over for? Is we about to do it?"

"Yeah, we about to do it, but it's not going to be just us?"

"What the hell you mean it ain't going to be just us?"

"It's going to be another girl involved. I'm almost six months pregnant. It's time for me to settle down. The only thing that I have never done is to have sex with two women at the same time. I'm about to have one last party and it includes you and Dianna."

"Dianna huh?" Renee did not have a problem with Dianna. They were never best friends, but they were alright with each other. She did not know if she would get turned on by Dianna, but if having a three way is what it was going to take to be able to have sex with Deidre, then she was like so be it.

Dianna arrived and she brought a bag of toys with her. She was surprised when she seen Renee sitting in Deidre's house.

"Hey girl," she said to Renee as she entered the living room.

"What's up Dianna?"

"I don't know, I just came to see what this crazy girl has up her sleeve."

"She didn't tell you?"

"No, I did not tell her." Deidre said cutting in, "But since you got a big mouth, why don't you tell her."

"She having an end it all party with us. We are going to have a threesome, and then she is going to settle down with my brother."

"Sounds like fun, I brought some of my toys." Dianna said pulling vibrators, the double headed dildo, handcuffs and anal balls out of her purse.

"Let's get this party started then!" she said excitedly.

"Come on let's move into the bedroom." Deidre told them. Her stomach was so big that she had to lean back when she walked into the bedroom.

When they got into the bedroom Deidre flopped down in a chair and said, "You two start the show." That was awkward for both Dianna and Renee. They had never had any sexual chemistry between each other and she wanted them to start the show off.

"What do you want us to do?" Dianna asked her.

"You can start by turning the stereo on and you two can do a striptease for me."

Dianna went over to the stereo and turned it on. She hit play and *Ginuwine's Greatest Hits* CD came on. The first song was Pony.

Dianna started dancing to the music seductively. She went over and stood in front of Deidre and started performing a striptease.

Renee saw all the attention that Deidre was giving to Dianna and was not about to be left out. She went over got next to Dianna and started performing her own striptease.

The girls danced side by side trying to outdo each other. They both were competing for Deidre's attention.

They were naked by the end of the first song. The next song was *So Anxious*. Renee fought for position, to get in front of Deidre. She got in front of her, and then turned her back to her. She bent over and grabbed her ankles and began wiggling her ass back and forth then she dropped it like it was hot.

Dianna went and got one of her vibrators. She laid on the floor, held her legs wide open up in the air and made her legs shake all the way down to her ass. Then she inserted the vibrator into her pussy, and began fucking herself with it.

She fucked herself slowly with the vibrator. She took two fingers and spread her pussy lips apart, so that Deidre could see how swollen her clit was. She licked her lips as she stared into Deidre's eyes.

Deidre started getting aroused. She wiggled out of her shorts and put both of her legs over the side of the chair and began fingering herself, "Go to her," Deidre told Renee.

Renee walked over to Dianna and dropped down. She removed Dianna's hand from the vibrator and took over. She fucked Dianna with the dildo. Dianna started moaning and gyrating her hips. They had finally made the connection.

Renee withdrew the vibrator from Dianna's pussy and stuck it in her own pussy. She would fuck herself for a moment then switch the vibrator back to Dianna's pussy.

"Get the double headed one." Deidre told them.

Dianna went and got the double headed dildo. She got down on her hands and knees, reached behind her and inserted the dildo into her pussy. Renee got down on her hands and knees, reached behind her and guided the other end of the dildo into her pussy.

They both started rocking back and forth on the dildo. Their ass would hit each other as they slammed onto the dildo. They slammed on it with so much force that their ass cheeks and titties shook every time they made contact. Dianna went into a zone. She started gyrating her hips on the dildo. She started talking saying Deidre's name.

"Yes Deidre! Fuck me baby. Oh yes fuck this pussy!" she had her eyes closed picturing Deidre in her head as the one that was fucking her.

Renee started cumming and she blurted out, "I love you Deidre. I love you so much."

Deidre felt that they had, had enough fun with each other. It was her party and time for her to have some fun.

She got up out of the chair and went over to the bed. She climbed onto it and turned to them.

"My turn girls, come give it to momma." They both got up off of the floor and went over to Deidre.

Dianna crawled onto the bed in front of Deidre and offered her, her titties. Deidre reached out and grabbed one. She pulled it to her mouth and began to suck on it like a newborn baby.

Renee picked up the same vibrator that had been used on her and Dianna and started fucking Deidre from the back with it. Being that Deidre was pregnant, her pussy was super wet. Renee would pull the vibrator all the way out of Deidre's pussy then put it back in. Every time she would pull it out, Deidre's pussy would make a popping sound.

Dianna leaned over top of Deidre, spread her ass cheeks and inserted a finger inside of her asshole. Deidre went crazy. She started bucking onto the finger.

Renee pulled the vibrator from her pussy and used her mouth to suck Deidre off. Dianna pulled her finger from Deidre's ass, took her hands and spread her ass cheeks, then started eating her ass. Deidre was having her pussy and ass ate at the same time. She had multiple orgasms.

For the rest of the night they shared Deidre. They would each have a part of her body at the same time. They even sucked both of her big toes at the same time. When they were sexed out they all fell asleep with Deidre in the middle.

Epilogue

Deidre had her threesome with Dianna and Renee, and then settled down with Roger. Roger moved in and two months later Deidre had a seven pound and two ounce baby boy.

The baby boy brought joy to a lot of people's lives. Deidre's father loved him as if he was his own son. Deidre's mother adored him and even with her and Deidre's disagreements she still did everything that she could for the baby.

Roger's mother was also delighted. Deidre started school back and had to resume working because Roger's disability could not cover all of the bills.

Renee moved in with them to help take care of little Earl. Everything was going beautiful for Roger. He had his girl, a son and him and his sister was closer than ever. One morning he got up early. It was a nice day and he decided to take the baby out in his stroller. He told Deidre that he was taking Earl to the park and would be gone for a couple of hours. She was still in the bed and told him that she was going to sleep in until they got back.

Roger left the house pushing Earl in his stroller. As soon as they were gone, Renee went into her bedroom. She pulled the covers back and Deidre was lying there naked. Deidre opened her legs and pulled them back. She told Renee. "Take your time eating this pussy. He is going to be gone for a couple hours." Renee went to sucking Deidre's pussy.

Roger had only made it to the corner before he realized that he had forgotten his wallet. He turned Earl's stroller around and headed back to the house. He got to the house, opened the door and wheeled Earl inside. He left Earl sitting in his stroller downstairs as he made his way up to the bedroom to get his wallet.

When he opened the bedroom door, his heart fell out of his chest and down into his stomach. There on the bed was his twin sister in between Deidre's legs eating her pussy as if that was her purpose in life.

"What the fuck are you doing!" he yelled at them. Shocked they both stopped and turned towards him. He stood there with tears in his eyes.

"I ought to kill you bitches. We are done Deidre. Renee never speak to me in life bitch!" Roger left out of the room and slammed the door shut behind him.

"What are we going to do?" Renee asked Deidre.

"What's done is done. We will worry about that later. Right now get back to sucking this pussy." Renee finished sucking Deidre's pussy then she returned the favor.

Roger ended up moving back home with his mother. Him and Deidre shared custody of little Earl. Roger and Renee stopped speaking to each other. She moved in with Deidre and together they continued on a sexual adventure that sometimes included men and sometimes included Dianna.

Deidre was grown and out on her own. She was no longer going to let anything or anyone come between her and her desires.

New Flavor Books & Publishing LLC

Book Order form

Full Name: _____

Institution# (If applicable):_____

Address: _____

Address 2: _____

City:_____ State:_____ Zip:_____

Book Title:	Price/Quantity
Hood to Hood: A Cleveland Story	**$15.00** ____
Hood to Hood 2: Spank's Revenge	**$15.00** ____
Tiffany's Addiction: Director's cut	**$15.00** ____
All Flavors A book of Erotic Short Stories	**$9.99** ____
Deidre's Desires	**$15.00** ____
Murder or Justice	**$15.00** ____
Hittin' Licks	**$15.00** ____
Gemini Killer	**$8.99** ____

Total Including ($3.00) Shipping and Handling _____

To place an order for one of our books please send a payment
for the price of the book plus $3.00 for shipping and handling to:

New Flavor Books & Publishing LLC

C/O Book orders

PO Box 603376

Cleveland, Ohio 44103

Please allow 2 - 4 weeks